I0553040

The Ultimate Con 2
Justice Is Served

The Ultimate Con 2 Justice Is Served

BY

TRACY WILSON

http://beautifulpublications.com

Published by
Beautiful Publications LLC
Stratford, CT 06614

PRINT ISBN: 978-1-7362753-4-4
EBOOK ISBN: 978-1-7362753-5-1

Printed in the United States of America

Dedication

This 1st series of 2021 is dedicated to my friends Snow & Flick. Thank you for agreeing to be written into my world.

CHAPTER ONE

"Who is it?" Flick asked as he heard a knock at the door...

"Room service..."

"We didn't order room service..."

"Compliments of the hotel..."

"Okay – I'll be right there..." Flick said as he got up to open the door...

"Get inside..." Bazil commanded. Flick looked down at the gun and did as he was told...

"Flick – who the – oh shit..." Sonovia said when she saw Bazil holding the gun. Sonovia got up off the bed and backed up next to Flick...

"That man you conned was my friend... and now... he's dead..."

"I didn't have shit to do with his death!" Flick exclaimed...

"You had everything to do with his death..."

"I didn't kill him!"

"He owed someone money... he couldn't pay them because you took his money... he's dead because of you..."

"Look – I'm sorry about your friend..."

"Sorry doesn't bring him back..."

"I know – I didn't know – I wasn't trying to get him killed..."

"Someone has to pay..."

"Here – take it!" Flick exclaimed as he threw the bag at Bazil...

"That's not enough..." Bazil said as he picked up the bag...

"That's all I got!" Flick exclaimed...

"That's not all you got..." Bazil said as he went over to Sonovia and pulled her to him...

"No... please... not my wife... take me..."

"Here..." Bazil said as he handed Flick an envelope...

"What's this?" Flick asked as he opened the envelope and took out a picture of Aiden. Flick's eyes got really wide...

"That's the man that killed my friend..."

"You want me to kill him?"

"I want him to pay for what he did to my friend..."

"How do I know you won't hurt my wife?"

"You don't..." Bazil breathed in Sonovia's ear and then he began kissing her on her neck...

2

"Take this..." Bazil said as he took a 9 millimeter with a silencer on it out his pocket and handed it to Flick...

"How am I supposed to know where to find him?"

"You have everything you need in your hand... and in that envelope..." Bazil answered as he took Sonovia's hand and led her towards the door...

"Are you hungry?" he asked as he took out his cell phone...

"No... no thank you..." she stammered...

"Are you thirsty?"

"I could use something to drink..."

"What's your preference?"

"Something to calm my nerves..."

"I have something in the limo you might like..." Bazil said as he continued to hold his cell phone. Sonovia followed him to the elevator without speaking. She was screaming inside but she didn't dare run because she knew if she ran, she'd never see Flick again... "Conrad..." Bazil spoke into the phone as they got in the elevator...

"Bazil! How are you?"

"You won't have a problem for much longer..."

"Is that right?"

"I'll talk to you soon..." Bazil said before he hung up and turned to look back at Sonovia... "After we get in the limo, I'll give you a drink... or

3

two... and then we're going for a ride..." he said as the doors opened and he walked her out. Bazil saw that she was shaking and he put his arm around her waist...

"Mr. Osgood! How are you?" the hotel manager beamed...

"I'm good..."

"And how are you Miss?" he asked as he inched closer to Sonovia...

"I'm fine..."

"Is your wife here?" the manager asked, thinking he was putting Bazil on the spot...

"I'll give her your regards..." Bazil said as he escorted Sonovia out to the limo. Bazil opened the door for her to get in and after she got in, he closed the door and went and got in on the other side...

"Where to Mr. Osgood?" Mike asked...

"The Grand Pequot..."

"Yes Sir..." Mike said as he drove off...

"Mike – we need a little privacy..." Bazil said. Mike closed the partition and Bazil spoke to Sonovia... "Pour yourself as much as you like..."

"Okay..." Sonovia said as she poured herself a half glass of Hennessey... "Oh Damn!" she exclaimed as she gulped it down...

"I guess you were thirsty..." Bazil laughed...

"The man called you Mr. Osgood..."

"That's right..."

"Are you Osgood Publishing?"

4

"Yes..."

"Oh shit!" she laughed... "I don't believe this shit – I read your books!"

"Thank you..."

"You're taking me to a hotel?"

"Yes..."

"Are we going to... have sex?"

"Would you like to have sex?"

"Hell no! – I mean... No... sorry..."

"Then we won't be having sex..."

"So... what are we going to do then?"

"Have another drink..."

"Okay..." she said as she poured herself another drink. Sonovia was scared to death but she wouldn't dare let him see that she was scared – and the fact that he wouldn't answer her question only made matters worse...

"We're here..." Mike said...

"Thank you Mike – I'll be back soon..." Bazil said as he got out and closed the door. Bazil went over to the other side, opened the door for Sonovia, helped her out, closed the door, and took her by the hand as he led her inside...

"Checking in?"

"Yes Maam..." Bazil answered...

"Name please?"

"Sonovia – she's talking to you..." Bazil said as he nudged her...

"Ummm... Sonovia Alexander..."

"That's a beautiful name..."

"Thank you..."

"You're all set – enjoy your stay..." the concierge clerk said as she handed Sonovia the room keys...

"What's your room number?" Bazil asked...

"543..."

"Right this way..." Bazil said as he took Sonovia by the hand and led her to the elevator. Bazil continued to hold Sonovia's hand as they got in the elevator along with another couple. The other couple got off on the 3rd floor and when the doors closed, Bazil looked Sonovia in her eyes. She wanted to look away but she was afraid of setting him off so she smiled instead...

"You have a nice smile..."

"Thank you..." the doors opened and Bazil led her off the elevator and down the hall to her room...

"Sonovia..."

"Yes?"

"The door won't open by itself..."

"Oh shit – sorry about that..." she laughed nervously as she opened the door...

"Nice room..." Bazil said as he went over to the bed and sat down. Sonovia stood there and watched Bazil turn on the television...

"I'm Della Crews, Anchor, News 12 Connecticut. We interrupt our regularly scheduled programming to bring you the following news. We now go live to Gwen Edwards. Go ahead Gwen...

"This is Gwen Edwards, Reporter, News 12 Connecticut. We're live at Mohegan Sun Casino. Earlier this evening an unidentified man was found dead in the men's room off the lobby on the south side of the casino. News 12 has just confirmed that the man has been identified as Sean Stewart. Police have no suspects at this time. We will continue to bring you updates...

"Umm... you stayin'?"

"Why?"

"Ummm... there's only one bed..."

"That's all we need..." Bazil said as he smiled at her mischievously...

"Ummm... I need to use the bathroom..." she said as she turned to go towards the bathroom...

"Sonovia..."

"Yes?" she answered as she turned around to face him...

"You need to take a shower..."

"Umm... I don't have anything to change into..."

"There's a robe and slippers in the closet..."

"Umm... okay..." she said as she went to the closet and took out the robe and slippers...

"I'll be here when you get out..." Bazil smiled. Sonovia didn't say anything – she turned

7

away from him, went into the bathroom, and turned on the shower...

"This man's gonna rape me – I know it..." she said out loud as she got in the shower... "Fuck it – I'ma take my time – I'ma wash my hair, blow it dry – I'ma try to stay in here as long as I can..."

"Hello?" Flick answered...

"How's it going?"

"Where's my wife?"

"She's in the shower..."

"If you hurt my wife – I'll kill you!"

"Call me back at this number and let me know when it's done..." Bazil laughed...

"Let me talk to my wife..."

"I already told you... she's in the shower..."

"How do I know she's in the shower?"

"Hold on..." Bazil said as he got up and went into the bathroom without knocking...

"AAAAGGGHH!"

"SONOVIA!" Flick yelled through the phone...

"Sonovia – Flick wants to talk to you..." Bazil said as he put the phone on speaker and stuck his hand behind the curtain so she could take the phone...

"Flick..." she whispered as she started crying...

"Did he hurt you?"

"No..."

"We gon' get through this – okay?"

"Okay..." she sniffed...

"I'll take my phone now..." Bazil said as he held out his hand. Bazil waited for Sonovia to hand him the phone and then he left the bathroom and closed the door behind him. He didn't speak to Flick again until he sat down on the bed... "I hope to hear from you soon..." Bazil said before he hung up. Sonovia was blow-drying her hair and Bazil waited patiently. When she came out of the bathroom, she walked towards the bed but Bazil stood up and went towards her before she had a chance to react... "Give me your phone..."

"Okay..." she said as she went to get her phone and handed it to him...

"I'm leaving now..."

"You're leaving?"

"Yes..."

"So I just wait here until you come back?"

"Yes..."

"Umm... I think I'm hungry..."

"Nice try..."

"I can't have anything to eat?"

"You can have whatever you like – the restaurant is open until 11 p.m. – use the phone – order room service – but whatever you do – don't leave this room – understand?"

"I understand..."

"Good – try and get some rest – you'll need it..." Bazil said as he left the room...

9

"Hello Conrad..." Bazil answered...

"How's it going?"

"The next 24 hours will tell us everything we need to know..."

"I don't think I can sleep..."

"I'm going to sleep like a baby..." Bazil said as he hung up...

"Where to Mr. Osgood? Mike asked...

"Home..."

"Yes Sir..." Mike said as he drove off. Bazil sat in the back of the limo, closed his eyes, and began rubbing his dick through his pants as he thought about Sonovia... "We're here..." Mike said, interrupting Bazil's thoughts...

"Thank you Mike – I'll call you in the morning..." Bazil said as he got out the limo and went inside...

"Daddy!" the kids said in unison when they saw him. Bazil didn't bother to take off his coat – he sat on the steps and let his children climb on his lap as he held them...

"I missed you Dad..." Jay said...

"I missed you too..."

"Did you miss me Daddy?" Joseph asked...

"I missed you all..." Bazil answered as he pulled them into a hug and held them...

"Daddy... you're choking me..." Joy laughed...

"Not me..." Lydia laughed as she held onto Bazil's waist...

"Where's your mother?"

"She's upstairs Daddy..." Lydia answered...

"I need to go upstairs to see your mother... and you kids need to go to bed..."

"Okay Daddy..." they all said in unison as they let go of him and followed him upstairs...

"Good night Daddy..." they all said in unison...

"Good night..." Bazil said as he went into the bedroom and closed the door...

"Are they gonna fight?" Lydia asked...

"I hope not..." Joy sighed...

"Jay! No!" Joseph exclaimed...

"I'm just gonna make sure they're not fighting!" Jay whispered as he tip-toed to their room...

"Where the hell have you been?" Beautiee snapped...

"I'm sorry..."

"I don't wanna hear how sorry you are..." Beautiee sighed as Jay listened outside their bedroom door...

"Beautiee..." Bazil sighed as he went over to her and pulled her into a kiss...

"I shouldn't have to ask Sam where you are..."

"I'm sorry..." Bazil breathed in her ear and then he began kissing her on her neck...

11

"Bazil..." she moaned...

"Yeesss..." he breathed as he kissed her again...

"Stop..."

"You don't want me to stop..." he breathed as he kissed her down to her breasts...

"Stop..."

"Okay..." he sighed. Bazil looked at Beautiee and pouted. Normally that would do the trick – but this time it didn't work...

"I love you..."

"I love you too..."

"You love me... but you don't trust me..."

"What do you mean?"

"We've been through a lot..."

"Yes... we have..."

"I died for you..." Beautiee whispered as she started to cry...

"Beautiee... No..." Bazil whispered as he started crying too...

"What do you need from me to prove you can trust me?"

"Beautiee... I'm not keeping anything from you... I promise..."

"Tell me where you were then..."

"I can't..."

"Let me see your hands..." Beautiee whispered as she took his hands in hers. Bazil sat still and let Beautiee explore his hands... "Your hands feel good..."

"Thank you..."

"I wasn't complementing you..."

"I don't understand..."

"Your hands are telling me you haven't killed anyone..."

"I haven't..." he breathed as he pulled Beautiee into a kiss and kissed her hard. Beautiee opened her mouth and welcomed his tongue and was completely unaware that Bazil was actually kissing Sonovia...

"They fighting?" Joseph asked as Jay came back into their room...

"Naa... they're playing..." he smiled. Joseph, Joy, and Lydia sat down on the floor as Jay turned on the television. After he turned on the television he climbed up on his bed and they got on the bed with him as he turned up the volume...

"Mmmph... Mmmph... Mmmph..." Beautiee moaned as Bazil pulled Sonovia's hair and pushed his tongue in deeper. Bazil stopped kissing her, stepped back away from Beautiee, took off his coat, and let it drop to the floor. Beautiee went over to Bazil, dropped to her knees, took his dick out his pants, and put it in her mouth...

"Yeeesss..." Bazil moaned as he imagined Sonovia sucking his dick. Bazil grabbed Sonovia's head and played in her hair as Beautiee took his dick all the way down her throat...

13

"Yeessss.... Fuuccckk!" Bazil moaned as he imagined Sonovia swallowing his dick... "Uuugh! Uuugh! Uuuugggghhhh!" Beautiee continued sucking his dick as Bazil imagined Sonovia was still hungry for more and before long, he was hard again... "Get up..." Bazil commanded. Beautiee got up and Bazil pushed her backwards towards the bed and pushed her down. Bazil imagined Sonovia on the bed in her robe and imagined her robe fell open as he snatched Beautiee's pants and panties off of her...

"Bazil..." Beautiee moaned...

"Open your legs..." Bazil commanded. Beautiee opened her legs, Bazil dropped down on his knees, and began to devour Sonovia...

"Bazil... Huh... Huh... Oh God..." Beautiee was moaning and trembling but Bazil was hearing and tasting Sonovia as she grabbed his head and came all over his face... "AAAAGGGHH! AAAAGGGHH! AAAAGGGHH!" Bazil was in a frenzy as he climbed up on Sonovia and slammed his dick inside her... "Bazil! Yes! Fuck me!" Bazil grabbed Sonovia's breasts and sucked them hungrily as he fucked her harder... "Yeesss! Fuck me!" Her moans added fuel to Bazil's fire and when he grabbed her ass and lifted her up with his hands they both lost it... "BBAAZZIILL! FUCK ME! I'M CUMMING!"

14

"UUGGHH! UUGGHH! UUUGGGHHH!" Bazil stayed inside Sonovia and began kissing her softly until Beautiee spoke...

"Oh my God..." she panted. Bazil opened his eyes, looked at his wife, and kissed her...

"You want more..." he breathed...

"Always..." she breathed. Bazil wasn't with Sonovia anymore. He was with his wife and, as she wanted, he was giving her more...

CHAPTER TWO

"There's that mutha fucka right there..." Flick said as he held the gun in his hand and aimed it... "Move Bitch!" he exclaimed as Mary approached Aiden and engaged him in conversation...

"Shit – at least the food's good..." Sonovia said as she ate. When she was finished, she pushed herself away from the table and got up... "I don't give a damn what he said – I ain't goin' to sleep – mutha fucka won't sneak back in here and take me..." she said as she pushed a chair across the room and pushed it up under the handle so the door couldn't be opened...

16

"Gotcha!" Flick said as he pulled the trigger. Flick watched as Aiden went down and waited...

"Oh my God!! Aiden!!" Mary screamed as she dropped down to her knees and hovered over him. Flick watched as she pulled out her phone... "Hello – he's been shot – he's not breathing – I'm in the parking lot at Mohegan Sun... I'm on level 6... Yes... Okay... Hurry!" she exclaimed as she cried. Flick was satisfied he was dead so he put the gun in his pocket before he went down the stairs. Flick made sure to check for camera's before he entered the parking lot so he knew he was in the clear. Once he got to the bottom level, he went into the casino lobby and made sure to bend his head down as he went into the men's room. When he got in the men's room, he went into the stall, changed his clothes, put the clothes in a duffel bag, cleaned the gun off, and put it in the duffel bag with the clothes. Flick put on plastic gloves, wiped down the bag with alcohol and sanitizer, put the bag on the floor, took the gloves off, and flushed them down the toilet as he heard a few men talking...

"My wife's gonna kill me..." one of them laughed...

"How much did you lose?"

"Two grand..."

"I gotchu..."

"You serious?!"

"Let's just say I had a good night..."

17

"Thanks man..." Flick waited for the men to leave and then he came out the stall, washed his hands, and left the bathroom...

"Excuse me..." the officer said as he tapped Flick on the shoulder...

"Yes officer?

"You need to have a mask on at all times..."

"Oh – sorry – my bad..." Flick said as he took his mask out his pocket and put it on his face...

"Good luck..."

"Thanks..." Flick said as he went into the casino...

"Shit – I'm tired – I'ma lay down on top of these covers in case I gotta jump up real quick..." Sonovia said as she lay down and began praying... "Lord... I know we fucked up... but please don't let him hurt my husband..." Sonovia fell asleep almost immediately...

Flick had been in the casino for a while and decided to go play a few hands of Black Jack. When he got to the table, he walked in on the following conversation...

"It happened about an hour ago..."

"Word?"

"He probably owed somebody money..."

"Sir?" the dealer asked, interrupting Flick's concentration...

"Oh – I'm in..."

"Very well – table's closed..." the dealer said as he dealt the cards...

"Hit or hold?" he asked Flick...

"Hold..."

"Dealer calls..."

"Shit!" one of the guys said as he threw down his cards...

"That's it for me..." another guy said. Flick watched as the dealer went from player to player, taking their money until he got to him...

"Twenty one!" Flick exclaimed...

"Beginner's luck..." One of the guys laughed...

"Dealer has 24 – congratulations..." he said as he gave Flick his winnings...

"I'm out..." Flick said as he left the casino and went to his room. As soon as he got in the door, he called his wife's phone...

"You have the wrong number..." Bazil answered...

"Where's my wife?"

"Bazil... who are you talking to?" Beautiee yawned...

"Go back to sleep..." Bazil breathed as he pulled Beautiee into a kiss. Flick was seething, believing that Bazil was in bed with his wife...

"Yo – it's done! I want my wife!"

"I'll see you tomorrow..." Bazil laughed as he hung up...

"Oh God... please don't let him hurt my wife..." Flick prayed...

"Yes Bazil..." Conrad answered...
"Your books are ready..."
"Thank you..."
"I'll send you the invoice now..."
"Got it – payment sent..." Conrad said as he turned on News 12...

"I'm Della Crews, Anchor, News 12 Connecticut. We interrupt our regularly scheduled programming to bring you the following news. We now go live to Gwen Edwards. Go ahead Gwen...

"This is Gwen Edwards, Reporter, News 12 Connecticut. We're live at Mohegan Sun Casino where it has been confirmed that a second murder has been committed here this evening. Aiden Holloway was shot and killed earlier this evening. His wife was with him when he got shot. She has no comment at this time. We will continue to bring you updates...

CHAPTER THREE

"Bazil?" Beautiee yawned...

"Go back to sleep..."

"Get back in here and put me to sleep..." Beautiee commanded...

"Beautiee..." Bazil breathed as he bent down to kiss her... "I need to go..."

"And I need to cum..." she commanded as she pulled Bazil down on top of her and spread her legs. Bazil took his dick out his pants and slammed his dick inside her...

"Is this what you want?" he growled...

"Yes... Fuck..." she moaned as she dug her fingers into his ass. Bazil kissed her hard, forcing his tongue in her mouth and Beautiee threw her pussy back at him as she sucked his tongue... "Huh... Huh... Huh..." Bazil loved it when Beautiee woke up like this... and so did his

21

dick as he began pounding her hard... "Fuck me Bazil! I'm cumming!"

"I'm cumming with you..."

"Aaagh! Aaagh! Aaagh! Aaagh! Aaagh!"

"Uuugh! Uuugh! Uuugh! Uuugh! Uuugh! Beautiee..." he breathed as she pulled him into a kiss and locked her legs behind his back... "I have to go..."

"Don't leave me... please..."

"I have to... I'm sorry..."

"Fine..." she sighed as she unlocked her legs and let go of him...

"Please don't be mad at me..." he breathed as he kissed her again and then he got up and left while the kids were still asleep...

"Good morning Mr. Osgood – where to?" Mike asked...

"Mohegan Sun..."

"Yes Sir..." Mike said as he drove off...

"We're here..."

"Thanks Mike – I'll be right back..." Bazil said as he got out the limo and went inside. As soon as he got inside, he saw Flick... "Good morning..."

"Good morning – where's my wife?"

"Come with me..." Bazil said. Flick followed Bazil out to the limo... "Get in..." Flick got in and closed the door. Bazil got in on the other side and closed the door... "Mike – we need privacy..."

"Yes Sir..." Mike said as he closed the partition...

"Where's my wife?"

"She's safe..."

"I did what you asked – I need to see my wife..."

"I'm a man of my word..." Bazil said as he pushed the intercom... "Mike – please take us to the Grand Pequot..."

"Yes Sir..." Mike said as he drove off and Flick noticed the duffle bag...

"Oh shit! What time is it?" Sonovia exclaimed as she jumped up and looked around... It's eight o'clock – I can't call Flick – Oh God – please let him be alright..." she prayed as she got up and went to the bathroom...

"We're here..." Mike said...

"Thanks Mike – you can take down the partition – I'll be back in a moment..." Bazil said as he opened the door, picked up the duffel bag, and got out. Flick didn't wait – he got out along with Bazil... "Come with me..." Bazil commanded. Flick followed Bazil through the lobby and onto the elevator. Bazil pushed the button for the 5th floor and Flick continued watching him closely and staring intently at the duffel bag...

"Go to your right..." Bazil commanded as the doors opened. Flick got off the elevator and did as he was told...

"This way?" Flick asked as he pointed to the right. Bazil nodded and Flick proceeded down the hallway...

"Stop right there..." Bazil commanded. Flick did as he was told... "Tell your wife to open the door...

"Sonovia!"

"Flick! Is that you?"

"Yea it's me – open the door!"

"Oh Flick – Thank God!" Sonovia exclaimed as she opened the door and Bazil pushed himself into the room behind Flick...

"Baby – you alright?"

"I'm alright..." she cried as they held each other...

"Did he touch you?"

"No..."

"I told you we gon' get through this!" he exclaimed as he kissed her...

"Oh my God – I thought I'd never see you again..." she cried...

"Ahem..." Bazil cleared his throat, interrupting their reunion... "We have unfinished business..." he said as he threw the duffel bag onto the bed...

"Yo – that's fucked up – I did what you asked – you didn't have to take the bag – I wiped it down – you could 'a left it there!"

"Open the bag..." Bazil commanded. Flick opened the bag and his eyes got really big...

"What's this?"

24

"That's your money..."

"I thought you said I had to pay for what I did..."

"I said someone had to pay for what happened to my friend... and they did..."

"So you never wanted the money..."

"I got what I wanted..." Bazil said as he turned to leave... "Oh – before I forget..." he said as he reached in his pocket and took out Sonovia's phone... "Here..." he said as he tossed her phone on the bed... "Check-out is at 12..." Bazil said as he turned and left...

"Oh shit – is he gone?" Sonovia asked as Flick ran to the door and locked it...

"He's gone..." Flick said as he pulled Sonovia into a kiss...

"Oh Flick..." she moaned as her robe fell open...

"I called you last night..." he breathed as he kissed her all over...

"I didn't have my phone..." she panted...

"He answered... he told me you were sleep... I heard a woman... I thought it was you..."

"Never Flick..."

"I imagined him touching you... it drove me crazy..." he said as he picked Sonovia up in his arms...

"I thought I'd never see you again..." she breathed as he lay her down on the bed, picked up the duffel bag, and dumped the money all over the bed...

"Flick – what are you doing?" Sonovia laughed...

"I've always wanted to do this..." Flick answered as he pushed Sonovia's legs open and took his dick out his pants...

"We're home..." Mike said as they pulled up...

"Yes we are..." Bazil said as he opened the door, got out, and closed the door... "Thanks Mike..." Bazil said as he waved and then he turned to go inside...

"Daddy!" the kids squealed when they saw him...

"Where's your mother?"

"She's upstairs Daddy..." Lydia beamed...

"Did you eat breakfast?"

"Jay gave us cereal..." Lydia answered...

"Good job Jay..."

"Thank you Daddy..." Jay beamed...

"I'm going to check on your mother..." Bazil said as he went upstairs...

"You're home..." Beautiee breathed as Bazil got in bed beside her...

"Yes Beautiee..." Bazil breathed as he got on top of Beautiee, opened her legs, and eased himself inside her... "I'm home..."

"Oh God... Yes... Fuck me Flick..." Sonovia moaned... "I'm cummin'... I'm cummin'..."

"I'm cummin' with you... I'm cummin' with you..."

"FFFLLLIIICCCKKK!"

"UUUUGGGGHHHH!" Flick lay there for a few moments until the phone rang... "Who the fuck is this?" Flick said as he answered the phone... "Hello?"

"This is the front desk..."

"I thought check-out was at 12 o'clock?"

"It is – we were just calling to confirm you didn't want a later check-out..."

"What time is the later check-out?"

"Two o'clock..."

"We'll take that..." Flick said as he began thrusting inside Sonovia again...

"We'll see you at two..." the clerk said as she hung up...

"You didn't hang up the phone..." Sonovia panted...

"I know..." Flick breathed as he pulled Sonovia into a kiss, pushed his tongue in her mouth, and fucked her harder...

CHAPTER FOUR

"Hey..." Bazil whispered as Beautiee opened her eyes...

"Hey..." she whispered back...

"I love you..."

"I love you too..."

"It sure is quiet..."

"Let's go see what they're up to..." Beautiee said as she got up...

"You takin' a shower?"

"Yea..."

"Can I come?"

"Again?" Beautiee laughed as she turned on the water and got in...

"Daddy!" Jay called as he knocked on the door...

"Comin' Jay..." Bazil said as he got up and opened the door...

"We're hungry..."

"We're coming..."

"Where's Mommy?"

"Mommy's in the shower..."

"Okay..." Jay said as he went back to his room...

"Are they fighting?" Lydia asked...

"No!" Jay laughed...

"I'm hungry!" Joy exclaimed...

"We're gonna eat as soon as Mommy gets out the shower..." Jay explained...

"C'mon – let's go downstairs and wait for Mommy..." Joseph said as they followed him downstairs...

"Is everything alright?" Beautiee asked...

"Everything's fine..."

"What did Jay want?" she asked as he came up behind her, grabbed her breasts, and began massaging them...

"He said they were hungry..." Bazil breathed as he eased himself inside her... "But he was really checking on us..."

"Huh... why... was... he... checking... on us..."

"To... ugghhh... see... if... we're... fucking..." Bazil growled as he fucked her deeper...

29

"Oh God... Bazil... Fuck me... I'm cumming..."

"Uuugh! Uuugh! Uuugh! Uuugh! Uuuggghhh!"

"Haah... Haah... Haah... Haah... Hhhaaahhh!"

"Now that you've fed me..." he breathed in her ear... "I'll let you go feed the kids..."

"I'll see you downstairs..." Beautiee laughed as she put on her robe, put on her slippers, and went downstairs...

"Good morning Mommy!" they all said in unison...

"Good morning..." she sighed...

"I'm hungry..." Joy exclaimed...

"What else is new? Beautiee laughed as she opened the refrigerator...

"Can we have omelets?" Jay asked...

"You can have whatever you want..."

"I want pancakes!" Joseph exclaimed...

"I want candy!" Lydia exclaimed...

"When you play candy land – that's when you'll get candy for breakfast!" Beautiee laughed...

"I want cereal!" Joy exclaimed...

"Omelets, pancakes, cereal, and candy? Are you sure you're going to eat all that?" Bazil laughed as he came into the kitchen...

"Daddy!" they all exclaimed in unison...

"Good morning..." Bazil said as he went over to them and kissed them on their foreheads... "Beautiee – what can I do to help?"

"Pick something!" Beautiee laughed as she prepared the omelets...

"Okay – let's see – we got honey nut cheerios, frosted flakes, and lucky charms – which one do you want?" he asked...

"Cheerios!" they all answered...

"Coming right up..." he laughed as he got four small bowls and poured a little bit of cereal in each one. The kids waited patiently as he took the milk out the refrigerator and poured it in the bowls. Bazil placed the bowls on the table and wondered why the kids were looking at him...

"Umm... Daddy?" Lydia asked...

"Yes Lydia..."

"We need spoons!" she laughed...

"Oh my God!" Bazil laughed. Beautiee laughed to herself as she put mini pancakes on the plates with the omelets and put the plates on the table...

"Thank you Mommy!" they all said...

"You're welcome..." she said as she put forks on the table so they could eat...

"Thank you Mommy..." Bazil said as he smiled at Beautiee mischievously...

"You're welcome Daddy..." she said as she placed a plate in front of him, gave him a fork, and sat down to eat with him...

"That's not your Daddy!" Lydia laughed. Bazil and Beautiee sat at the table, watching the kids as they ate. When they were finished, Jay put the dishes in the dishwasher and made sure the table was clean...

"Thank you Jay..." Beautiee said...

"You're welcome Mommy..." he said as and then they all went into the living room. Jay turned on the television and was just about to change the channel when Beautiee stopped him...

"Jay – leave it!"

"I'm Della Crews, Anchor, News 12 Connecticut. We interrupt our regularly scheduled programming to bring you the following news. We now go live to Gwen Edwards. Go ahead Gwen...

"This is Gwen Edwards, Reporter, News 12 Connecticut. As we confirmed yesterday, Sean Stewart and Aiden Holloway were found dead at the Mohegan Sun casino. Sean Stewart's body was discovered in the men's room near the entrance on the South side of the casino. News 12 has just confirmed that the cause of death was his neck being snapped. Aiden Holloway was shot and killed in the parking lot on the 6th floor of the Sky Tower. Police are in the process of reviewing the surveillance videos and have no suspects at this time. We will continue to bring you updates...

Beautiee looked at Bazil and saw tears in his eyes... "Okay Jay – you can change it..." she said as she got up from the table and went into the library. Bazil came into the library and closed the door... "That's where you were last night..."

"I didn't kill him..."

"I know you didn't..."

"How do you know?"

"Because..." she answered as she went to him and pulled him into a hug... "I saw your pain..." Bazil burst into tears and cried on her shoulder...

"I couldn't save him... I tried... but I couldn't..."

"I'm sorry..." Beautiee whispered as she held him...

"All he had to do was get the money and he'd still be alive..."

"Come here..." Beautiee said as she took his hand, led him to the couch, and sat down. Bazil sat beside her...

"I love you so much..."

"I love you too..."

"He called me..."

"Okay..."

"He was conned..."

"Oh..."

"I told him I would help him get his money back..."

"Okay..."

"I tracked them down..."

"Uh huh..."

"I told him where they were..."

"They were in the casino..."

"All he had to do was get his money – but he listened to the wrong head – and it got him killed..."

"I don't understand..."

"He went to their room..."

"Uh huh..."

"The money was in the safe..."

"Ooohhh..."

"He got his money..."

"Okay..."

"I was waiting downstairs..."

"What happened?"

"He wanted her..."

"Who?"

"His wife..."

"I don't understand..."

"I knew something wasn't right... I went upstairs... I burst into the room... he was in bed with her..."

"Oh my God! Did he rape her?"

"He was going to – but I stopped him – I hit him – I told him to grab the money... we went downstairs..."

"Where was her husband?"

"He couldn't stop him... he had a gun..."

"Oh my God... Bazil... you saved her..."

34

"I saved her... but I couldn't save him..." he whispered as he started crying again...

"I thought he got the money?"

"He grabbed the wrong bag..."

"What?"

"He grabbed the wrong bag... he didn't have his money..."

"Bazil... I'm sorry..."

"He had to pay for what he did..."

"You just told me you didn't kill him..."

"I didn't..."

"Look at me..." Beautiee commanded as she picked up his face by his chin. Bazil looked directly at her as she searched his eyes. When Beautiee smiled at him, he knew they were going to get through it...

"God I love you..." he breathed as he pulled her into a kiss and kissed her hard...

CHAPTER FIVE

"I wish we didn't have to check out..." Sonovia sighed...

"We can come back..." Flick said as he got up...

"We've been through some shit..." she said as she got up...

"I know one thing – I don't wanna see any melatonin..."

"I know that's right – le'me flush this shit down the toilet..." she said as she took the bottle out the nightstand and went into the bathroom...

"Babe – whatchu doin'?"

"I'm flushing this shit down the toilet..." she laughed as she flushed...

"Now the fishes can go night night..."

"Ain't no damn fishes here!" Sonovia laughed...

"Well wherever the water goes – whoever drinks it can go to sleep..." Flick laughed as he got in the shower...

"You stupid!" Sonovia laughed as she got in the shower with him...

"Don't start no trouble – we don't have time for that..."

"You better make time for it..." she said as she pulled him into a kiss...

"Welcome home..." Flick said as he carried her into the house..."

"Not for long..."

"I can't wait for us to buy the house..."

"Me either..."

"Snow... can we talk?"

"Yea..." she said as she sat down on the couch. Flick sat down beside her...

"What did Bazil do when... you know..."

"Nothing..."

"You were in the shower..."

"We got in the limo; he told the driver we needed privacy..."

"Okay..."

"He told me to pour myself as much as I wanted..."

"Oh so you were drinking?"

"I had one strong drink – and it was nasty!"

"Did he have a drink?"

"No..."

37

"So you had a drink – then what?"

"I asked him if he was taking me to a hotel..."

"He told you he was?"

"Yea..."

"So he didn't drug you?"

"No Flick..."

"Okay wait – he took you in the limo – he told you to pour yourself a drink – then he tells you he's taking you to a hotel – this shit don't make sense..."

"I asked him if we we're gonna have sex – he asked me if I'd like to..."

"WHAT?!"

"I told him hell no!"

"What'd he say?"

"He said if I didn't want to have sex – then we wouldn't have sex..."

"What the fuck – this doesn't make sense – I heard you in the shower – you were crying..."

"I was scared Flick..."

"I know Baby – I'm sorry – I'm just trying to figure this shit out – he didn't touch you at all?"

"He had his arm around me when we left the casino and he held my hand in the elevator – once we got in the room he just sat on the bed..."

"How did you wind up in the shower?"

"He told me I needed to take a shower..."

"I heard you scream..."

"He scared me..."

"He told you to take a shower – you go take a shower – did he touch you when he came in the bathroom?"

"No..."

"What happened when you got out the shower?"

"He told me to give him my phone..."

"That's it?"

"That's it..."

"So he took your phone – and left?"

"I gave him my phone – he told me he was leaving – I asked him if I was supposed to stay there until he got back – he said yes – I told him I was hungry – he said I can order whatever I want but make sure I don't leave the room – he asked me did I understand – I said I understand – he left..."

"So who the fuck was he with when I called your phone?"

"I'on know – but it wasn't me..."

"He planned this shit!"

"You think so?"

"I know so – that's why he didn't want the money..."

"I don't think so Flick..."

"What do you think?"

"He was mad as hell at Sean – especially when... you know..."

"Oh shit!"

"What Flick?"

"He didn't touch you because he didn't want you..."

"Duh!"

"You don't get it..." Flick laughed...

"Okay – I don't get it..."

"He was mad at Sean because Sean didn't take the money and leave..."

"What are you saying Flick?"

"Bazil told Sean get the money – let's go – you and me wasn't supposed to be in it..."

"Flick?"

"Yea?"

"Sean is dead..."

"I know that!"

"Flick – Bazil said somebody had to pay for what happened to his friend..."

"The envelope..."

"What was in the envelope Flick?"

"I... I can't..."

"Flick..." Sonovia said as she touched his face... "Tell me..."

"I can't Baby... I can't..."

"Why not? Don't you trust me?"

"I'm protecting you..."

"Protecting me? From what?"

"I don't want him to come back..."

"Flick... nobody's coming... he didn't hurt me... he doesn't want to hurt me... he wouldn't even let Sean hurt me..."

"You're right... but I still can't tell you what was in that envelope..."

40

"Flick... you love me... don't you?"

"Baby..." he breathed as he kissed her... "You know I love you..."

"And you know I love you – and you won't tell me what was in that envelope..." she said as she started crying...

"Baby please..." he said as he kissed her... "Don't cry..."

"I need to know what happened – I couldn't call you – I was scared to death – I thought he was going to hurt you just like you thought he was going to hurt me..." she cried...

"Aiden..." Flick sighed...

"Aiden? You had to kill Aiden?"

"I had to..." he sighed...

"Damn Flick! What the fuck am I supposed to do without you?"

"Baby – I'm sorry – see – this is why I didn't wanna tell you – and you're not gonna be without me..."

"I will if you get caught..."

"I'm not gonna get caught..."

"Flick – they have cameras all over the casino..."

"I know that..."

"So what makes you think you won't get caught?"

"Bazil gave me everything I needed in that envelope..."

"You wasn't supposed to kill Aiden..."

"Yes I was..."

"Flick – listen to me..."

"Okay..."

"Sean was supposed to take the money and go – but he took the wrong bag..."

"That's right..."

"If he took the right bag – he'd still be alive – and Aiden would be dead – but he took the wrong bag..."

"You think Sean was supposed to kill Aiden?"

"One of them was supposed to kill Aiden – and it wasn't supposed to be you..."

"Oh shit!"

"Guess who Bazil is?"

"Who is he?"

"Osgood Publishing..."

"WHAT?! Sonovia – do you know who that is?"

"Nigga I just told you who he is!" she laughed...

"Sonovia – that nigga killed his first wife – and Beautiee went to jail for trying to kill him, his boyfriend, and her girlfriend!"

"I know you lyin'!"

"His son-in-law is the sergeant that works at the precinct where he got arrested!"

"Oh shit – I told him I read his books – I don't remember reading this shit!"

"You ever read In The Arms Of A Gangster?"

"No..."

"That's Beautiee's Biography – she told it all – she writes books too – and she was on Oprah!"

"Le'me go download these books – I don't believe this shit!"

"One of them put a hit out on Aiden..."

"Damn – I really like Mary too – she gonna call me cryin' 'n shit – I gotta comfort her 'n shit..."

"I know..."

"I'm not worried now..."

"You not?"

"Naa – if this nigga gangster like you say – he won't bother you – he didn't even take the money..."

"He doesn't need it..."

"Flick?"

"Yea?"

"How'd you do it?"

"I'm not telling you that..."

CHAPTER SIX

"Good morning Detective..." Officer Walker said...

"Good morning..." Katina replied...

"I've been reviewing the surveillance from the casinos..."

"You mean casino..."

"I mean casinos..."

"What are you telling me?"

"See for yourself..." he said as he showed her the footage...

"Is that who I think it is?" she asked as her eyes got really big...

"That's who you think it is..."

"Oh my God – I could kiss you!"

"If you wanna kiss me after watching this one – I can only imagine what you'll want to do to me after you watch this one..." he said as he showed her the second video..."

"No! He's cheating on Beautiee?"

"He left Mohegan with her in the first video... he showed up with her in the second video..."

"Even if he's not cheating – this is good!"

"Can I get that kiss now?"

"Boy bye!" she laughed as she left the precinct..."

"Hello Katina..." Chandler said as she walked in...

"Hello Chandler..."

"May I speak to you in private?"

"Sure..." he answered as he came out from behind the desk... "I'll be in my office..." he said and then Katina followed him inside and closed the door... "What can I do for you?"

"You've seen News 12 – right?"

"About the two murders at the casino?"

"Yes..."

"I've seen it – why?"

"We've reviewed the surveillance... and... look – I'ma just say it..."

"Say what?"

"Your father-in-law is a person of interest in both murders..." Chandler bust out laughing... "Chandler – this isn't funny!"

"Wait... stop... I can't..." he laughed...

"Look – I came here as a courtesy – I could 'a just went straight to him..."

"Are you charging him?"

"Not yet..." she said as she walked out...

"Hello Chandler..." Bazil answered...

"Hi Dad..."

"What's wrong? Is Starr okay?"

"She's fine..."

"Are the kids okay?"

"Yea..."

"What time are you going to lunch?"

"12..."

"I'll meet you at Thelma's..." Bazil said and then he hung up... "Beautiee?"

"Yes Bazil?"

"Can I see you for a minute?"

"You can see me for as long as you like..." she answered as she got up from her desk and went over to him...

"Chandler called..." he sighed...

"I'll call Smalls..."

"Don't call him..." he said as he pulled her into a hug and held her...

"What can I do for you?"

"You're already doing it..." he breathed as he kissed her...

"I love you..."

"I love you too..."

"What time are you leaving?"

"11:30..."

"Will I see you later?"

"Yeeesss..." he breathed as he kissed her again...

"Oh – excuse me..." Sam said as he came in...

"Sam – I'm leaving for the day..."

"Okay..."

"If you need anything – run it by Beautiee..." he said as he left...

"Did you need something?" Beautiee asked...

"Never mind..." Sam said as he turned and left...

"Welcome to Thelma's – hello Sergeant!" she exclaimed when she saw Chandler...

"Hello..." he replied...

"You meeting your father for lunch?"

"Yes I am..."

"Oh good – I can't wait to see him!" she exclaimed as Bazil walked in... "Hello Mr. Osgood – your son is waiting for you..." she gushed...

"Good afternoon – thank you..."

"I'll bring you some sweet tea..." she said as she went to get a pitcher of tea..."

"Hello Chandler..." Bazil said as he sat down at the booth..."

"Hello Dad..."

"Let's see – mac & cheese, collard greens, and fried chicken wings – right?" the waitress asked as she put the sweet tea on the table with two glasses with ice and poured them both a glass...

"Right..." Bazil answered...

"I'll go get that right now..." she said as she went to place the order...

"Katina came to see me..." Chandler sighed...

"I guess I'll be seeing her soon..."

"Here you go – enjoy!" the waitress said as she put the plates on the table...

"Thank you..." Bazil said...

"You're always welcome..." she sighed...

"Thank you..." Chandler said...

"You're welcome Sergeant..." she smiled...

"Should I be worried?" Bazil laughed as they started eating...

"My heart belongs to Starr..." Chandler answered...

"Glad to hear it..."

"I wish I had a friend or a brother to fix her up with..." Chandler laughed...

"Is she annoying you?" Bazil laughed...

"Oh no... not at all..." They both continued eating without speaking...

"Thanks for lunch..." he said as he got up...

"You're welcome Dad..." Chandler said as Bazil left...

CHAPTER SEVEN

"Welcome to the Holiday Inn – are you here to check in?"

"Yes I am..." Mary answered...

"Name please?"

"Mary Holloway..."

"Ms. Holloway – I see you're booked for 30 days?"

"I'm booked for 30 days for the time being..."

"I hope you enjoy your stay with us..."

"I hope so too..." she sighed...

"Here you go – you're in room 313..." Virginia said as she handed her the room keys...

"Is the pool on that floor?"

"Yes it is..."

"Thank you..." Mary said as she went to the elevator... "I can't wait to get in my room and unwind..." she said out loud as she went down the hall. As soon as she opened the door, she put the 'Do Not Disturb' sign on the door... "Nice, clean, and comfortable – just like I like..." she said as she took her clothes out the suitcase and hung up her clothes in the closet... "Now to get down to business..." she said as she left the room, went downstairs, and left the hotel...

"Hello, how may I help you?" Chandler asked as she walked into the precinct...

"I'm looking for information regarding my husband's death..."

"What's your husband's name?"

"Aiden Holloway..."

"Come with me..." Chandler said as he stepped from behind the desk... "I'll be in my office..." he said as Mary followed him... "I'm Sergeant Corbett..." he said as he sat down...

"My name is Mary Holloway..."

"I'm sorry for you loss..."

"Thank you..."

"I'm afraid I don't have much to tell you at this time..."

"Let me be the judge of that..."

"Your husband was killed at Mohegan Sun..."

"Yes, I know..."

"I think you should go talk to Detective Jones..."

"Why?"

"She has more information regarding your husband's death – she works out the 3rd precinct in Milford..."

"Thank you – I'll do that... but I do wish you could tell me something..." she sighed as she got up to leave...

"I can tell you they have a person of interest..."

"Really? Who?"

"I can't really tell you – it hasn't been made public yet..."

"Sergeant... please... I don't have anybody to talk to... I'm all alone... I... I don't think I can hold it together... I miss him so much..." she cried on cue...

"Here..." Chandler said as he passed her some tissues...

"Thank you..." she sniffed...

"Bazil Osgood..."

"Bazil Osgood?"

"He's the person of interest..."

"Thanks – but that man didn't kill my husband..." she said as she got up and left...

"Yes Chandler..." Bazil answered...

"Do you know Mary Holloway?"

"That's Aiden's wife..."

"How do you know her?"

51

"Are you asking me as a Sergeant?"

"She just came to see me..."

"Thank you..." Bazil said as he hung up...

"What time is the next train?" Mary asked out loud as she looked at the schedule... "Ten minutes – good – I can make it..." she said as she got on the elevator. Mary got her ticket just as the train was pulling in... "Perfect..." she said as she got on the train and sat down...

"Ticket please..." the conductor said. Mary gave him her ticket and he gave it back to her... "You'll be there in about 15 minutes..." Mary sat and looked out the window as the train moved. She looked out at the water and got sad as she thought about her husband...

"Milford next..." came over the speaker. Mary got up, got off the train, and decided to walk to clear her mind as best she could under the circumstances...

"Hello – may I help you?" Sergeant Hurley asked...

"I'm looking for Detective Jones..."

"I'm Detective Jones..." Katina said as she walked into the lobby... "How can I help you?"

"I need to speak to you about my husband..."

"Who's your husband?"

"Aiden Holloway..."

"Come with me..." Katina said as Mary followed her... "I'm sorry for your loss..."

"Thank you..."

"How can I help you?"

"I actually came here to help you..."

"Help me?"

"Yes..."

"I'm all ears..." Katina said as she sat down...

"I understand Bazil Osgood is a person of interest in my husband's death..."

"You spoke to Chandler..."

"Who's Chandler?"

"Sergeant Corbett – go ahead..."

"Ms. Jones..."

"Katina..." she interrupted...

"That's pretty..."

"Thank you..."

"Bazil didn't kill my husband..."

"If that's true, the evidence will prove that..."

"Before my husband was killed, he told me somebody owed him money and they didn't have the money to pay him..."

"Do you mind if I record our conversation?"

"You can if you like..."

"Thank you..." she said as she took out a mini-recorder... "This is Detective Katina Jones, 3rd Precinct, Milford, Connecticut. Today is Friday, December 18, 2020. The time is 4:15 p.m. I'm sitting here with Mrs. Holloway – she came to

53

see me and she has given her consent to have this conversation recorded – Mrs. Holloway – I need you to repeat what you just told me..."

"Before my husband was killed, he told me somebody owed him money and they didn't have the money to pay him..."

Did he tell you who owed him money?"

"No..."

"When did he tell you this?"

"He told me this before we went to dinner."

"Where did you have dinner?"

"We had dinner at Ballo on Tuesday night..." Mary said as she got choked up. Katina handed her some tissues...

"Are you okay to continue?"

"Yes..."

"Go ahead..."

"While we were having dinner, my husband got a call on his cell phone..."

"Do you know who it was from?"

"No..."

"Did he say anything?"

"He didn't say anything but... he... he..."

"What's wrong Mrs. Holloway?"

"I told him I was glad he took the call... because he was happy..." she sniffed... "He even asked me if I was jealous..." she laughed...

"Were you?" Katina laughed...

"No – but I was curious..."

"I bet..."

"He told me he was getting paid later that night..."

"So you had dinner, he got the call, he was happy, you were happy... what happened after that?"

"We had another drink; we went upstairs... and..." Mary sat there smiling as she reminisced about their evening...

"Did your husband stay with you for the night?"

"No – he went back down to the casino – he had a thing for the tables..."

"What time did he come back upstairs?"

"I'm not sure... 2 a.m.... 3 a.m...."

"What time did you check out?"

"We checked out at 12..." she answered as she got chocked up again. Katina passed her some more tissues... "We went to the parking lot... and... I'm sorry..." she said as she started crying. Katina got up, went over to her, hugged her, and let Mary cry on her shoulder for a few moments... "I'm sorry..."

"You don't need to apologize..." Katina said as she got up... "I wanna show you something..." she said as she took the laptop out of her desk, went back over to Mary, sat down beside her, and opened it...

"What's this?"

"Look..." Katina said as she showed Mary the surveillance...

"Aiden..." she sighed...

"Do you know this man?" Katina asked as she pointed to Sean..."

"That's the man that was killed the night before my husband was killed...

"This is Bazil..." Katina said as she pointed to him...

"Yes... I know..."

"He's following Sean and your husband to the men's room..." Katina said as she pointed to the screen. Mary watched intently. She gasped when Aiden came out and Sean didn't... "Oh my God – did Aiden kill Sean?"

"We think so..."

"Why?"

"We can't prove it... but we think maybe Sean was supposed to pay Aiden and didn't..."

"That doesn't make any sense! It was only $45,000! We don't need the money!"

"Wait – are you saying your husband was expecting a payment of $45,000?"

"Yes..."

"You said you don't need the money..."

"Aiden told me our mortgage was paid off last month – we have rental properties – we have store fronts – it doesn't make sense!"

"Your husband's a gambler..."

"Yes he is..."

"Is it possible he owed someone money?"

"No..."

"Look at this again..." Katina said as she replayed the surveillance... "You see where Bazil is listening at the door?"

"Yes..."

"See how he backs away before your husband comes out?"

"Yes..."

"We think Bazil set Sean up to be killed... and we think he set your husband up to be killed..."

"No..."

"Mrs. Holloway – I know you don't wanna believe that but..."

"My husband isn't a killer, Bazil didn't set Sean up to be killed, and he didn't set my husband up to be killed..." Mary said as she got up to leave...

"Mrs. Holloway – wait – please..." Mary sat back down... "I want you to look at this..." Katina said as she played the surveillance of Bazil leaving with Sonovia...

"Oh my God – that's Snow!"

"Who?"

"That woman – that's Sonovia Alexander..."

"How do you know her?"

"We met at I-Hop in Yonkers..."

"Yonkers?"

"We met in Yonkers. We had breakfast and then I found out we were both staying at the Hyatt in Cross County..."

57

"Did you see her at Mohegan Sun?"

"No... I didn't..."

"Thank you Mrs. Holloway – you've been very helpful..." Katina said as she smiled. Mary sat there thinking... "Is there something else?"

"It's nothing..." Mary lied...

"Let me be the judge of that..."

"Well... before we went to the restaurant, I played Wheel of Fortune – Progressive..."

"Did you win?"

"I won $20,000..."

"Congratulations..."

"I told my husband I wished Snow was there... and now I see she was there... and she left with Bazil..."

"I wanna show you one more thing..." Katina said as she played more surveillance... "This is at Foxwoods..."

"Bazil's going into the casino with Snow..."

"This is a few hours later..." Katina said as she showed Mary another video...

"He's leaving by himself..."

"Look at this surveillance..." Katina said as she showed Mary a video of Flick at Mohegan Sun...

"Why would Flick let Snow go off with Bazil?"

"This is the surveillance from where your husband was killed..." Katina said as she showed Mary the video...

"Aiden..." she whispered as she started crying...

"As you can see – we have no idea who the killer is – all we got on surveillance is his shoe..." Katina said as she zoomed in on the shoe. Mary put a tissue up to her face and pretended to cry as she smiled to herself...

"I wish we had more..." Katina sighed...

"I appreciate you taking the time to show me this..."

"This surveillance shows Flick and Bazil going into Foxwoods the next morning..." Katina pointed out... "And this one shows Bazil leaving the casino by himself..."

"This doesn't make any sense..."

"How do you know Bazil Osgood?"

"We sold him the building where his publishing company is located..." Mary answered as she got up to leave...

"May I have your phone number if I have any more questions?"

"I'm staying at the Holiday Inn in Bridgeport – room 313..." Mary answered as she left...

CHAPTER EIGHT

"Hello – may I help you?"

"I'm here to see Bazil Osgood..."

"Name please?"

"Mary Holloway..."

"One moment..." Shadaijah said as she called Bazil...

"Yes Shadaijah?"

"There's a Mary Holloway here to see you..."

"Thank you Shadaijah – please bring her to the conference room..." Bazil said before he hung up...

"Beautiee..."

"Yes?"

"Come with me..." he said as he got up. Beautiee followed him and they went down to the conference room...

"Hello Mary..." Bazil said...

"Hello Bazil, Hello Beautiee..."

"Mary... do I know you?" Beautiee asked...

"Your husband bought this building from us..." Mary explained...

"Nice meeting you – can I get you some coffee?"

"Do you have anything stronger?" Mary laughed...

"We have Strawberita's and Limearita's..." Beautiee beamed...

"You let your employee's drink on company time?"

"Nobody really drinks on company time – and if they have something while they're at lunch, there isn't enough alcohol in it to be an issue..." Beautiee laughed...

"I'll have a Limearita..." Mary said...

"I'll be right back..." Beautiee said as she went to the cafeteria...

"We have a problem..." Mary said...

"I know..."

"You know?"

"Chandler called me..."

"Sergeant Corbett?"

"He's my son-in-law..."

"Wait – what – never mind – that's not why I'm here..."

"I know that too..."

"Here you go..." Beautiee said as she came back with two glasses of limearita's with straws, a Heineken, and a glass. Mary waited for Beautiee to put them on the table...

"Thank you – can we talk?" Mary asked...

"We can talk..." Bazil answered...

"I came here to find out who killed my husband..."

"Oh my God! Your husband was killed?" Beautiee asked...

"My husband was killed at Mohegan Sun..."

"Oh no! Who was your husband?"

"Aiden Holloway..."

"I'm sorry..."

"Thank you – I just came from speaking to Detective Jones..."

"Katina..." Bazil sighed...

"Oh so you know her?"

"Intimately..." Beautiee laughed...

"Intimately? I don't understand..."

"It's a private joke – go ahead..." Bazil said...

"I was told you were a person of interest in my husband's murder..."

"Mary... I..."

62

"Bazil – I know you didn't kill my husband..."

"Oh thank God!" Beautiee exclaimed...

"But for some reason, this detective thinks you had something to do with it..."

"Doesn't surprise me..." Bazil said...

"They have a lot of surveillance..."

"I see..."

"One of the videos shows you following Sean to the men's room – that's why they think you set Sean up to be killed by my husband..."

"Mary..."

"Bazil – I know..."

"Sean was my friend..." Bazil sighed...

"So he owed my husband money..."

"Yes..."

"And my husband didn't pay him..."

"I don't know..." Bazil sighed. Mary watched as Beautiee got up from the table and came over towards her...

"Stand up..." Beautiee commanded...

"Excuse me?"

"I said stand up..."

"Look – I don't know what type of game you're playing – but I want nothing to do with it!" Mary snapped as she stood up to leave and Beautiee grabbed her around her waist and pulled Mary against her... "Let go of me!"

"I will... as soon as I'm sure you're not wearing a wire..." Beautiee said as she ran her hands down Mary's back to her ass. Mary stood still and allowed Beautiee to feel her across her breasts and back down to her waist...

"Satisfied?"

"Satisfied..." Beautiee said as she stepped away from Mary and Mary sat back down. Beautiee sat back down next to Bazil and finished her Limearita...

"Sean told me he owed Aiden $45,000. I met him at the casino to make sure he paid your husband the money. I followed them to the men's room. Next thing I know... he's dead..." Mary looked at Bazil's face. She knew Bazil was telling the truth...

"They have another video that show's you leaving with Snow..."

"Who's Snow?" Beautiee asked...

"Sonovia Alexander. She's an author..." Bazil answered...

"What were you doing with her?" Mary asked...

"Sean tried to rape her..." Bazil sighed...

"How could Sean try to rape her after he was already dead?"

"He tried to rape her before he died..."

"How do you know this?"

"I saw him..." Mary sat there, sipped on her limeratia, and thought. Beautiee and Bazil watched her intently...

"Bazil – in all these years - you haven't changed a bit!" she laughed...

"What do you mean?"

64

"You just can't be satisfied with one woman..." she laughed...

"Mary – it's not what you think..."

"Bazil – you may have your wife fooled – no offense Beautiee – but you don't have me fooled – you left with her so you could fuck her!" she laughed...

"Mary – let's say for argument's sake what you're saying is true – it isn't – but let's just say that it is – what does that have to do with the death of your husband?"

"Bazil Osgood – I don't believe it..."

"Mary – what are you talking about?"

"Let me spell it out for you..."

"Please – I'm all ears..."

"You were played..."

"Huh?"

"Somebody wanted my husband dead..."

"Okay..."

"Snow and Flick played us both..."

"Mary – you lost me..."

"I met them in Yonkers at I-Hop... we had breakfast... I found out we all stayed at the same hotel... at the same time... next thing you know – you show up to make sure Sean pays my husband... Snow pretends to be a damsel in distress and needs to be rescued... you rescue her... Flick has the opportunity to kill my husband... he goes back to his room... next morning you pick him up and bring him to his wife... and they're so appreciative that they make sure the surveillance makes you the person of interest in both murders..."

"Oh shit!" Beautiee exclaimed...

"I have to say – I never thought of it like that – but you're wrong about Snow..." Bazil said...

"I don't think so..."

"What makes you say that?"

"Snow showed me how to play the slot machines. We really hit it off. Flick invited us to his room for drinks. Next thing you know – we're so drunk we both fell asleep – and we had to be brought back to our room in a wheel chair..."

"Oh my God – were you drugged?" Beautiee asked...

"My husband believes we were..."

"What happened after you woke up?" Beautiee asked...

"We went to their room but they were in the shower, so went back to our room and waited for them to call us. My husband asked them both what happened and they both insisted that we were drunk and fell asleep. I laughed it off but my husband kept telling me something wasn't right – and now that he's dead – I know something wasn't right..."

"How can you be sure?"

"Katina showed me the surveillance from the night my husband was killed..." she said as she started choking up. Beautiee got up, got a box of tissues, handed it to her, and sat back

66

down... "They don't know who the killer is... but they could see his foot... and when Katina zoomed in on the foot... I recognized the shoe..."

"Mary... I'm sorry..." Bazil said...

"I'm sorry too – but don't worry – if they try to come after you I'll defend you..."

"Thank you Mary – I appreciate it..."

"Mary – can I ask you something?" Beautiee asked...

"Sure..."

"You didn't tell Katina that you know Flick killed your husband – did you?" Mary didn't answer Beautiee's question. She finished her drink, got up from the table, and smiled...

"It was nice seeing you again Bazil – nice meeting you Beautiee..." she said as she left the conference room, went down the hall, and left the building. Beautiee got up from the table, walked over to Bazil, pulled him close to her, and looked in his eyes. Beautiee smiled when she got the answer she was looking for...

CHAPTER NINE

"Hi..." Chandler sighed...

"Hey..." Starr said as she pulled him into a hug... "What's wrong?"

"Daddy!" Lil' Chandler squealed...

"Hey..." Chandler said as he picked his son up...

"I missed you Daddy!"

"I missed you too... where are your sisters?"

"They playin'..." he answered as he Chandler put him down and he ran down the hall... "Daddy's home!" he yelled...

"Hi Daddy!" they yelled from their room...

"Hi!" Chandler yelled back...

"Why didn't you just go say hello to them?" Starr laughed...

"Cause I like yellin'!" he said as he pulled Starr into a hug and started tickling her..."

"Chandler... stop..." she laughed...

"Make me..." he breathed as he kissed her...

"Chandler... don't stop..."

"Ooohhh... okay..." he laughed as he started tickling her again...

"Chandler... stop..." she laughed...

"Make up your mind..." he laughed...

"Okay... okay... stop..." she laughed...

"Okay... I'll stop..." he laughed...

"Now..." she said as she wrapped her arms around his neck... "Tell me what's wrong – and don't tickle me..."

"You saw the story about the men that were killed in the casinos?"

"Yes..."

"Your father was there..."

"Chandler..."

"Katina came to see me... he's a person of interest..."

"Is my father going to be arrested?"

"I don't know..."

"Hey Beautiee..." Keisha answered...

"Can you get the kids?"

"You good?"

"No..."

"I'll talk to you when you get here..."

"Thank you Keisha..."

"Bazil!" Smalls answered...

"I need your help..."Bazil said...

"I got time..."

"We're on our way..."

"Come in..." Smalls sighed...

"Hey..." Beautiee said as she hugged him...

"Hey Beautiee..."

"Hey..." Bazil sighed as he sat down

"What's going on?"

"Katina..."

"What now?"

"The murders at the casino..."

"Bazil – I swear to God..."

"Smalls – No!"

"Okay... what are their names?" Smalls said as he pulled out a legal pad and started writing...

"Sean Stewart, Aiden Holloway..."

"Got it – go..."

"Sean was my friend..."

"Okay..."

"He told me he owed Aiden money. He got his money back at the casino. I met him there to make sure he paid Aiden. I followed them to the men's room... next thing I know... Aiden comes out... Sean doesn't..."

"Katina thinks you set him up..."

"Yes..."

"Did you?"

70

"Smalls..."

"Answer the question..."

"No..."

"I'm sorry... I have to ask... Was Beautiee with you?"

"No..."

"So you went there to meet Sean to make sure he paid Aiden... Did he pay him?"

"I don't know..."

"But he was found dead in the men's room..."

"Yes..."

"Did you go in the men's room to check on your friend?"

"No..."

"You knew he was dead... didn't you?"

"Yea..."

"How'd you know he was dead?"

"I heard Aiden call him a stupid mutha fucka..."

"So you didn't go check on your friend?"

"No..."

"Damn..."

"There was nothing I could do..."

"Did you leave?"

"I left... with Sonovia..."

"Who's Sonovia?"

"She's an author..."

"You left the casino with another woman... and your wife was at home?"

"Yes..."

"Beautiee – you knew about this?"

"Yes..."

"Why were you with her?"

"I went to check on her..."

"Bazil... you need to tell me everything..."

"I know..."

"Well?"

"He tried to rape her..."

"Who?"

"Sean..."

"Did she report it?"

"No..."

"Bazil... I need to ask you a question..."

"I know..."

"What was Sean doing in the room with her?"

"They had his money..."

"They? Who the hell is they?"

"Sonovia and Flick..."

"Who's Flick?"

"Her husband..."

"You knew they had his money..."

"Yes..."

"He was supposed to get the money and pay Aiden – but he wanted to have sex with her first..."

"I stopped him..."

"So you went to check on her..."

"Yes..."

"And you left the casino with her..."

"Yes..."

"Where did you go?"

"Foxwoods..."

"You went to check on his wife... you left with his wife... you took his wife to another casino... and?"

"We checked into the hotel..."

"Bazil! What the fuck is wrong with you?!"

"I went home to my wife..."

"Beautiee – is that true?"

"Yes..."

"Did Flick know where his wife was?"

"He was gambling..."

"So you just took his wife to another hotel... checked her in... and left?"

"Yes..."

"Aiden was killed at Mohegan Sun..."

"I know..."

"You were home with your wife..."

"That's right..."

"So why does Katina think that you set Aiden up to be killed?"

"I'm not sure..."

"Did you go back to the casino?"

"I went back the next day..."

"You went back the next day? Why?"

"I spoke to Flick – he didn't know where his wife was – I picked him up – I took him to his wife..." and I left them both at Foxwoods..."

"So... you did all that because you were concerned about his wife?"

"I felt guilty..."

"I thought you said you left her alone?"

"I did..."

"Why did you feel guilty?"

"It's my fault..."

"What's your fault?"

"It's my fault he tried to rape her..."

"How is that your fault?"

"I told him where they were..."

"Now I get it – you knew they had his money – you told him where they were – he didn't come downstairs with the money – you went upstairs to get him – you saw him trying to rape her – you stopped him – Bazil – that's not your fault..."

"He's dead because of me..."

"No he isn't..." Beautiee said as she hugged him...

"Beautiee's right – you had nothing to do with them taking Sean's money – you had nothing to do with what happened in the men's room..." Smalls said...

"Why didn't he just pay him? He had the money – why didn't he just pay him?" Bazil said as he broke down...

"Bazil – it's alright – we gotchu..." he said as Beautiee held him and Smalls got up, came from behind the desk, and sat down on the other side...

"His wife came to see me..."

"Whose wife came to see you?"

"Aiden's wife..."

74

"What's her name?"

"Mary Holloway..."

"Hold on..." Smalls said as he got up, went back to his desk, and wrote the name down...

"Katina told her I was a person of interest..."

"How – you know what – never mind – I'll talk to her later – what else did she say?"

"They have a lot of surveillance..."

"What do they have?"

"One of the videos shows me following Sean to the men's room..."

"You shouldn't have talked to her – she could've been wearing a wire..."

"She wasn't..." Beautiee said...

"Are you sure?"

"She felt good..." Beautiee laughed...

"Oh shit – that's what I'm talkin' about – okay!" Smalls laughed...

"They have another video that show's me leaving with Snow..."

"Is that it?"

"They also have surveillance from Foxwoods..."

"I got it – cheating doesn't make you a murderer..."

"I didn't cheat on my wife..."

"I know you didn't – Beautiee knows you didn't – but Katina won't believe it – doesn't matter though..."

"Mary told me something else..."

"Tell me..."

"Mary believes Snow and Flick set Sean up, they played me, and made it look I'm responsible for the murders... and now that I've spoken to her... I believe her..."

"How can you be sure she's telling you the truth?"

"Mary met them in Yonkers at I-Hop. They had breakfast – and then she found out they were all staying at the Hyatt in Yonkers..."

"That could just be a coincidence..."

"Mary said Snow showed her how to play the slot machines. Flick invited them to their room for drinks. Next thing you know – they were so drunk they both fell asleep – and they were brought back to their room in a wheel chair..."

"They were drugged..."

"Her husband believed they were..."

"What else did she say?"

She said they went to talk to them but they were in the shower so they waited for them to call – they spoke to Snow and Flick - they both insisted that they were drunk and fell asleep – Mary laughed it off Aiden kept telling her something wasn't right..."

"And now her husband's dead..."

"Snow played the damsel in distress to rescue her so Flick would have the opportunity to kill Aiden..."

"She might be right..."

"Katina also showed her surveillance from the night her husband was killed..."

"Did she see anything?"

"They have a man's foot – but that's all they got..."

"Bazil..."

"No Smalls – it's not my foot – it wasn't me!" Bazil laughed...

"Okay – I have everything I need – you may be a person of interest – but you're definitely not a murder..." Smalls said as he put the pad in his desk drawer and locked it...

"Thank you..." Bazil said as he got up...

"You're welcome..." Smalls said as he got up...

"Thank you..." Beautiee said as she hugged him...

"You're welcome..."

"I love you..." Bazil said as he hugged Smalls...

"I love you too..."

"I'll keep you posted..." Bazil said as they left Smalls' office...

CHAPTER TEN

"Mommy! Daddy!" they squealed when the saw their parents...

"Uncle Bazil! Auntie Beautiee!" Amina squealed...

"Woooaaa!" Bazil boomed as he squatted down for the kids to hug him and they knocked him to the floor...

"I don't know why he lets them do that..." Keisha laughed...

"He does the same thing with his grandkids..." Beautiee laughed...

"Y'all good?" Troy asked...

"Let's wait for Bazil..." Beautiee sighed...

"Oh boy – c'mon..." Keisha said as Beautiee followed her into the living room.

"Y'all go upstairs..." Troy said...

78

"Okay!" they squealed as they ran upstairs...

"I'm glad you called Beautiee – Amina's been driving us crazy!" Troy laughed...

"Really?" Bazil asked as he got up off the floor and sat on the chair...

"Really!" Keisha laughed...

"Keisha – you can always send Amina to our house..." Beautiee said...

"I'ma pack her shit so you can adopt her..." Keisha said...

"No you not either..." Troy laughed...

"You must be carrying another girl..." Beautiee said...

"It's not 'cause I'm pregnant – it's 'cause she miss y'all..."

"Aww... we're sorry Keisha..." Bazil said...

"What's goin' on wich'all?" Troy asked...

"We had to go see Smalls..."

"What'd you do this time?" Keisha laughed...

"According to Katina – I set those guys up to be killed..." Bazil laughed...

"Wait – what guys?" Troy asked...

"Sean Steward and Aiden Holloway..."

"The guys that were killed at the casino?" Keisha asked...

"Yea..." Beautiee answered...

"I swear – God gave y'all the right careers..." Keisha laughed...

"What makes you say that?" Bazil asked...

"Y'all can write books for the rest of your lives..." Keisha laughed...

"Well you're not in jail so maybe they figured it out..." Troy said...

"Aiden's wife went to see Katina..." Bazil said...

"Oh shit!" Troy exclaimed...

"She told Katina I didn't kill her husband..."

"How you know she told her that?" Keisha asked...

"She came to see us earlier..." Beautiee answered...

"Somethin' ain't right..."

"I know..." Bazil agreed...

"Wait a minute – Bazil – what did you do?"

"I went to the casino..."

"So why are you being singled out?"

"Because they saw me with Sean and Aiden..."

"Oh shit – you hang out with us all the time – should we be worried?" Troy asked as they all laughed...

"I'm Della Crews, Anchor, News 12 Connecticut. We interrupt our regularly scheduled programming to bring you the following news. We now go live to Gwen Edwards. Go ahead Gwen...

"This is Gwen Edwards, Reporter, News 12 Connecticut. We have been communicating with police departments in Bridgeport as well as Milford regarding the deaths of Sean Stewart and Aiden Holloway at Mohegan Sun. Detective Jones from the 3rd Precinct in Milford has issued the following statement:

"We are continuing to gather evidence and we are still in the process of reviewing surveillance. No arrests have been made, and we have no suspects at this time."

"I'm Gwen Edwards, Reporter, News 12 Connecticut. We will continue to bring you updates. We now return to our regularly scheduled programming. Back to you Della..."

"Glad I got that out the way..." Mary said as she went inside...

"Welcome to Park City Grill – how may I help you?" the hostess asked...

"I'd like to place an order to go..." Mary answered...

"What would you like?"

"I'd like coconut shrimp, buffalo wings, and the open-faced grilled salmon..."

"Okay – it'll be about 15 minutes..."

"I'll be at the bar..." Mary said as she went and sat down...

"What would you like?" the bartender asked...

"I'll have a tequila pomegranate sour..."

"Coming right up..." Mary sat there and started thinking about Aiden. When the bartender gave her the drink, she remembered their last dinner together...

"Well Aiden – it's not as good as Ballo's – but it'll do..." she sighed...

"How's everything?"

"Good..." Mary answered as she continued sipping. The truth was nothing was good because her husband was gone...

"Excuse me – your food's ready..."

"Thank you..." Mary said and then she gulped down her drink and went to pay for her food...

"Would you like to charge this to your room?"

"Yes please..."

"Okay – just sign here, put your room number, and you'll be all set..."

"Thank you..." Mary said as she signed the receipt, took her food, and went upstairs. As soon as she got in her room, she turned on News 12 to see if there were any updates...

"I'm Della Crews, Anchor, News 12 Connecticut. We interrupt our regularly scheduled programming to bring you the following news. We now go live to Gwen Edwards. Go ahead Gwen...

"This is Gwen Edwards, Reporter, News 12 Connecticut. We have been communicating with police departments in Bridgeport as well as Milford regarding the deaths of Sean Stewart and Aiden Holloway at Mohegan Sun. Detective Jones from the 3rd Precinct in Milford has issued the following statement:

"We are continuing to gather evidence and we are still in the process of reviewing surveillance. No arrests have been made, and we have no suspects at this time."

"I'm Gwen Edwards, Reporter, News 12 Connecticut. We will continue to bring you updates. We now return to our regularly scheduled programming. Back to you Della..."

"Hmmm... I thought they would be announcing that Bazil was a person of interest..." she said as she shrugged her shoulders... "Oh well – doesn't matter – I got what I wanted..." she sighed as she sat at the table and started eating... "I wish they would show the surveillance – that would make for interesting television – but I guess Bazil doesn't really deserve that..." she sighed as she continued eating.. "Shoot – I should've gotten something to drink... maybe they have something in here..." she said as she opened the refrigerator... "Oh well isn't this nice..." she said as she looked in the refrigerator and saw two bottles of water, a Heineken, and a Pepsi... "I'll wash this down with Pepsi..." she said as she took the Pepsi out the refrigerator, sat back at the table, poured herself some in the cup, and called Sonovia...

"Hi Mary – I'm so sorry..."

"Thank you Snow..."

"I would've called you sooner, but we just got home..."

"Were you at Mohegan Sun?"

"Yes we were..."

"I wish I knew you were there! We had dinner at Ballo!"

"We did too!"

"I wanted to share my good fortune with you..."

"Tell me..."

"I won $20,000..."

"Oh my God! That's great!"

"I remembered what you told me..."

"I'm so happy for you!"

"Thank you Snow..."

"Have you made any arrangements yet?"

"Not yet – they still have my husband's body..."

"Oh wow..."

"I don't mind – I want them to take as much time as they need to bring my husband's killer to justice..."

"Exactly..."

"I'm staying here in Bridgeport..."

"Bridgeport, Connecticut?"

"Yes – I'm at the Holiday Inn..."

"How long will you be staying?"

"I'm checked in for 30 days... for now..."

"Why so long?"

"I wanted to be close to the precincts in Bridgeport and Milford – this way if they need to talk to me – I'm in close proximity..."

"I know that's right – have you spoken to the police yet?"

"I spoke to them earlier today..."

"Really? I can't believe they called you already..."

"Oh they didn't call me – I showed up in person..."

'I know that's right – did you find out anything?"

"They had surveillance from the night Aiden was killed..."

"They caught it on video?"

"Oh yea..."

"Have they arrested anybody?"

"Not yet – but they won't be making an arrest anytime soon..." Mary sighed...

"Why not?"

"The killer's body wasn't caught on camera – but his foot was..."

"I know you lyin'!"

"I know – right?" Mary laughed...

"I can't believe all they got was a foot..."

"Snow... that's not all they got..."

"What else did they get?"

"They have surveillance of you... leaving Mohegan Sun... with Bazil Osgood..."

"Bazil? Oh yea – it was good seeing him..."

"So you know Bazil?"

"Oh yea – I read his books..."

"I'm a little tired – I've had a long day – I'll give you a call tomorrow sometime - I downloaded your books so I'll have something to read..."

"You downloaded my books?"

"Yes – you could've told me who you were Snow..." Mary laughed...

"I like when I meet people and they like me for me – this way I know it's genuine..."

"I understand. I'm glad I got to know you before I knew who you were – but now I'm going to start reading one of your books and find out who you really are!" Mary laughed...

"Okay Mary – if you need anything – call me..."

"Thanks Snow – good night..." Mary said as she hung up... "Don't forget to kiss your husband goodbye..." she said as she took her kindle out of her purse and started reading Liar Liar...

"Oh Shit!" Sonovia exclaimed...

"Hey babe – what's wrong?"

"Mary's in Bridgeport..."

"Connecticut?"

"She checked into the Holiday Inn for 30 days..."

86

"That's nice – you goin' to see her?"

"Flick – that's not nice – she talked to the police..."

"So what?"

"So they showed her surveillance from the night her husband was killed..."

"So?"

"Mary said they got the killer's foot in the video!"

"Oh shit!"

"Did you change your shoes?"

"Yea I changed my shoes!"

"Do you still have those shoes Flick?"

"Yea..." he sighed...

"Where's the damn shoes?!"

"Right there in the closet..." Sonovia got up and went in the closet...

"These are the shoes?"

"Yea..."

"I'll be right back..." she said as she opened the door, went into the hallway, and threw the shoes into the incinerator... "Them shoes will be burned tomorrow!" she exclaimed as she slammed the door and sat back down...

"You want a drink?"

"I need a drink – especially after what else she told me..."

"Le'me get you a drink – and a shot..."

"I don't want a shot..."

"Take the shot with me Babe..." Flick said as he handed it to her... "To us..."

"Whatever..." she said as she gulped it down... "Damn! What is it with men and nasty liquor?!"

"What are you talkin' about?" Flick laughed...

"This that same shit Bazil had in the limo!"

"Oh so you were drinkin' Hennessey..."

"I guess so..."

"What else did Mary have to say?" Flick asked as he handed her a drink...

"She said they have a video of me leaving the hotel with Bazil..."

"Oh shit! What the fuck did you say?!"

"Calm down Flick – I told her it was good seeing him again..." she laughed...

"Oh so she thinks you know Bazil?"

"Oh yea – I told her I read his books – and she told me she's reading mine..."

"Oh so she knows who you are?"

"If she didn't know who I was before – she's about to find out!" she laughed...

CHAPTER ELEVEN

"Huh... Troy... Fuck..."

"Keisha... Oh shit... Keisha..."

"Harder..."

"I'on wanna... hurt... the... baby..."

"I swear... to... God... if you don't... give me... that... dick... I'ma... scream..."

"You want this dick?" Tory growled as he fucked her harder..."

"That's what the fuck I'm talkin' about!" Yes! Fuck me!"

"Keisha... I'm..."

"Fuck me! I'm cumming!"

"Oh shit... Fuck..."

"Aaaahhhhh!"

"Uuuugggghhhh!"

"Thank you Daddy..." she panted... "I needed that..."

89

"Mommy got that Good Good..." Troy panted...

"I know that's right..."

"Can I get some more?" Troy breathed in her ear...

"As long as the door is locked... you can get as much as you want..." she breathed as she pulled him into a kiss and they went for round two..."

"Mommy can Amina spend the night?" Joy asked...

"Sure she can..." Beautiee answered...

"I need to ask Mommy!" Amina exclaimed...

"I already told your mother you could stay..." Beautiee said...

"You did?"

"Yes Amina..."

"Yea!" the girls squealed as they ran upstairs...

"What are you going to do when Keisha calls you and tells you to send Amina home?" Bazil laughed...

"They're not going to call us..."

"How can you be so sure?"

"I know how it is when you're pregnant..." Beautiee laughed...

"You wanted the dick in the hospital..." Bazil breathed as he pushed her down on the couch, got on top of her, and started kissing her...

90

"I couldn't wait to get home..." she breathed as they continued kissing...

"As I recall... you didn't wait..." Bazil breathed as he kissed her...

"Daddy?" Jay interrupted...

"Yes Jay..." Bazil sighed as he sat up...

"I just wanted to say good night..."

"We'll be up in a minute..." Bazil said as he got up... "C'mon..." he said as he helped Beautiee up and they went upstairs...

"We're going to bed Daddy..." Joseph said as he got in the bed...

"Good night..." Beautiee said as she kissed him on his forehead...

"Good night Mommy... I love you..."

"I love you too..." Bazil kissed Jay and then went to kiss Joseph as Beautiee kissed Jay...

"Good might Mommy... I love you..."

"I love you too..."

"I love you both..." Bazil said...

"We love you too Daddy..." When they got to the girls room the girls were already in bed watching television...

"I set the timer Daddy..." Joy said. Bazil and Beautiee kissed them all good night...

"I love you..." Beautiee said...

"Love you too!" they all said...

"I love you..." Bazil said...

"Love you too! They all said as Amina started laughing...

"Amina – why are you laughing?" Beautiee asked...

"I like spending the night over your house – when it's time for me to go to bed at home, Mommy tells me git your ass in the damn bed!"

"Why does Auntie Keisha do that?" Lydia asked...

"Cause I don't listen..." Amina answered as they all laughed. Beautiee and Bazil started to go down the hallway to their room as the phone rang...

"I bet I know who that is..." Beautiee said as she hurried to get the phone... "Hey Keisha..."

"Can Amina spend the night?"

"She's already in bed..." Beautiee laughed...

"She's already in bed? Girl – how the fuck – never mind – good night!" she said as she hung up...

"Was that Keisha?" Bazil asked...

"Yea..." Beautiee laughed as Bazil closed the bedroom door...

"Katina – it's late – I wanna go home..." Beverly sighed...

"I know – I wanna go home too – but something's not right..."

"Look Katina – I wanna get Bazil as much as you do – but there just isn't enough evidence to charge him..." Beverly sighed...

"I know..."

"You agree with me?"

"Yes..."

"What's the problem then?"

"Mary came to see me..."

"Aiden's wife – I know – I read her statement..."

"She made sure I knew she didn't believe Bazil killed her husband..."

"Because he didn't!" Beverly exclaimed...

"Exactly..."

"Katina – what are you getting at?"

"She knows who killed her husband..."

"What makes you say that?"

"She's staying at the Holiday Inn in Bridgeport..."

"That's not surprising..."

"She told me she checked in for 30 days..."

"Why so long?"

"I think somebody put a hit out on her husband... and she's here to take out the hitter..."

"If you were anybody else – I'd say you were crazy..."

"So you don't think I'm crazy?"

"I've worked with you long enough to know you're not..."

'I'm going to call Bazil in for questioning..."

"Why? We don't have enough to charge him..."

"We don't need to charge him..."

"Why are we questioning him then?"

"Because he's a person of interest..."

"He's not the murderer Katina..."

"He's not the murderer – but he knows the deceased..."

"How?"

"Mary told me they sold him the property where his publishing company is located...

"He's been in Milford nearly 10 years..."

"Exactly..."

"Katina – I'm tired... and I have a dick appointment..."

"Why is Mary reaching out to Bazil after nearly 10 years – unless he's buying another property?"

"That's a good question..."

"I'll call Bazil tomorrow..."

"Good – I'm tired – I'm hungry – and I'm horny – I'll see you tomorrow..."

"Good night Beverly..." Katina laughed...

"Is that your phone?" Beautiee yawned...

"Yes Smalls..." Bazil answered...

"Tomorrow morning at 10..."

"Where?"

"Her office..."

"We'll be there..."

CHAPTER TWELVE

"Good morning – does anyone need coffee?" Katina asked..."

"We all need coffee..." Beautiee laughed...

"We can go into the other room and you can help yourself if you like..."

"Thank you..." Beautiee said as she got up... "Honey – I'll get your coffee..." she said to Bazil as she started to leave...

"I'll be right back..." Smalls said as he got up and they went into the kitchen area...

"You don't mind leaving your husband alone with Katina?" Smalls asked...

"Naa... I get a kick out of it..." Beautiee laughed as they made their coffee. When they were finished, they brought their coffee back into Katina's office and sat down... "Here..." Beautiee said as she handed Bazil a cup of coffee...

95

"Thank you..." Bazil said...

"Thank you for coming in..." Katina said...

"You say that as if I had a choice..." Bazil laughed...

"Let me start by saying that I asked you to come in for questioning – you're not under arrest and you're not being charged..."

"Is my client a person of interest?" Smalls asked...

"Yes... and no..." Katina answered...

"Is this conversation being recorded?" Smalls asked...

"Not by me..." Katina laughed. Smalls sat there and smiled. There are cameras as you can see – but that's surveillance – we're not recording anything – but I will be taking notes, just as you'll be taking notes..."

"That's fine..." Smalls said...

"Bazil – I called you down here for questioning because I met with Mary Holloway – and I have additional questions after reviewing her statement..."

"You have additional questions to the questions you were planning to ask me?" Bazil laughed...

"Exactly..."

"This is gonna be good..." Smalls said...

"Mary said before her husband was killed, he told her somebody owed him money and they didn't have the money to pay him. She also said while they were at dinner, her husband received

96

a call and he was happy because he was told he would be getting paid..."

"Do you have a question for my client?" Smalls asked...

"Yes I do..."

"Okay – go ahead..."

"Bazil – we've reviewed the surveillance videos from Mohegan Sun and we saw you with Sean Stewart..."

"That's not a question..." Smalls said...

"Did Sean Stewart tell you he owed Aiden Holloway money?" Bazil looked at Smalls. Smalls nodded...

"Yes..." Bazil answered...

"I wanna show you something..." Katina said as she put her laptop on the table so everyone could see it... "This is the surveillance of you and Sean... here's where you're following Sean and Aiden to the men's room... you're listening at the door... and then you back away from the door right before Aiden comes out..."

"Do you have a question for my client?" Smalls asked...

"Yes I do..."

"Go ahead..."

"Did you set Sean up to be killed?"

"No..."

"Why were you listening to what was going on in the men's room?" Bazil looked at Smalls. Smalls nodded...

"I wanted to make sure Sean was okay..." Bazil sighed...

"I want you to have another look at this surveillance..." Katina said as she rewound it and played it back. This time, Katina zoomed in on Bazil's face... "You were hurt..." she said...

"Do you have a question for my client?" Smalls asked...

"Yes I do..."

"Go ahead..."

"Did you know what was going to happen in the men's room?"

"No..."

"Did you see where Aiden went when he came out the men's room?"

"No..."

"So – to be clear – you don't know what happened in the men's room?"

"I don't know what happened – but I heard something..." Smalls looked at Bazil and raised his eyebrow...

"What did you hear?"

"When Aiden came out the men's room he called Sean a stupid mother fucker..."

"How did you know Sean owed Aiden money?"

"He told me..."

"So you knew Sean?"

"He was my friend..."

"I'm sorry..."

"Thank you..."

98

"Did you see where Aiden went after he came out the men's room?"

"No..."

"I have another video I'd like to show you..." Katina said as she played the surveillance showing Bazil leaving the casino with Sonovia... "Who is this woman?"

"That's Sonovia Alexander..."

"How do you know her?"

"What does that have to do with anything?" Smalls asked...

"I'm getting to that..." Katina answered...

"She's an author. She introduced herself to me and told me she's read some of my books..." Bazil answered...

"I wanna show you another video..." Katina said as she played more surveillance... "This is you... going into Foxwoods with Sonovia..."

"Do you have a question for my client?" Smalls asked...

"Not yet...." she said as she played another video... "This is you... leaving Foxwoods..."

"Do you have a question for my client?" Smalls asked...

"Not yet..." she said as she played another video... "This is the surveillance from where Aiden Holloway was killed..." Katina said as she showed zoomed in on the killer's foot... "As you can see – we have no idea who the killer is – all we got on surveillance is his shoe..."

"Do you have a question for my client now?" Smalls asked...

"Yes I do..."

"Finally! Go ahead!"

"Bazil – what size shoe do you wear?"

"I wear a man's 9..."

"May I take a look at your foot?"

"Would you like me to put it up on the table for you?"

"That won't be necessary..." Katina said as she started playing another video...

"What's this?" Smalls asked...

"This surveillance shows you and Sonovia's husband going into Foxwoods the next morning..." Katina pointed out... "And surveillance shows Bazil leaving the casino by himself..."

"Do you have a question for my client?" Smalls asked...

"I have a few questions..."

"Go ahead..."

"Do you know why Sonovia left her husband to go with you?"

"I can't swear to it... but I would say she came with me because she wanted to..." Katina looked at Beautiee. Beautiee looked at Katina and smiled...

"Did you spend the night with her?"

"No..."

"So you went home?"

"I went home..."

"Beautiee – is that true?"

"Absolutely..." Beautiee sighed...

"What made you go back to Mohegan Sun, pick up her husband, and bring him to Foxwoods?"

"It was the least I could do..."

"I don't understand..."

"I would be livid if my wife left me in the casino and went off with another man – I'd want answers – and I'd want the man she left with to answer them..."

"Hmmm... I see..." Katina said as she sat there thinking and tapping her pen on her legal pad...

"Do you have any other questions for my client?" Smalls asked...

"Yes I do..."

"Go ahead..."

"Did you see Mary at the casino?"

"No..."

"Have you seen Mary since her husband was killed?"

"Yes..."

"When did you see her?"

"I saw her yesterday..."

"So you met with her..."

"I didn't meet with her – she showed up at my office..."

"You had no idea she was coming to see you?"

"No..."

"Hmmm... interesting..." she said as she sat there thinking and tapping her pen on her legal pad again...

"Do you have any more questions for my client?" Smalls asked...

"Yes I do..."

"Go ahead..."

"What did Mary want to see you about?"

"She told me everything you discussed..."

"Could you be more specific?"

"Mary told me you questioned her about Sean, her husband, me, and she let me know you had the surveillance..."

"Did she accuse you of killing her husband?"

"No – in fact, she told me she knew I didn't kill her husband..."

"She said that? Those were her exact words?"

"Yes..."

"Hmmm... interesting..." she said as she sat there thinking and tapping her pen on her legal pad again...

"What are you thinking Katina?" Smalls asked...

"Mary told me that they sold you the building where your publishing company is located in Milford..."

"That's correct..." Bazil said...

"So when you saw Mary yesterday – that was the first time you've seen her in about 10 years..."

"That's correct..."

"Hmmm... interesting..." she said as she sat there thinking and tapping her pen on her legal pad again...

"What's so interesting?" Smalls asked...

"I'm going to show you something..." Katina said as she pulled up another video...

"What's this?" Smalls asked...

"This is Mary checking out at 12 the next day..."

"What does that have to do with my client?" Smalls asked...

"I think somebody made sure your client showed up to the right place... at the right time..."

"What?"

"Your client hadn't seen Mary in nearly 10 years... he shows up at the casino... Mary's at the casino... her husband's at the casino... your client's friend is killed... her husband is killed... she doesn't check out until the next day..."

"What does that have to do with my client?"

"Somebody wanted to make it look like your client set this up... somebody wanted us to look at your client... if my husband was killed – I wouldn't be able to sleep – I'd be at the police station..."

"What are you saying?" Smalls asked with a smile...

"Bazil – would you be willing to do something for me?" Bazil looked at Smalls...

"That depends on what you want my client to do..."

"If Mary contacts you again – let me know..."

"Why would my client do that?"

"Never mind..." Katina said as she put her pen in her jacket, closed the laptop, and got up from the table...

"Did I do something to offend you?" Smalls asked...

"No – not at all..." she answered as she picked up the laptop, picked up the notepad, put them in her desk drawer, and locked it...

"Do you need my client for anything else?"

"No – thank you for coming in – have a good day..." she said as she left her office in a hurry...

"What was that all about?" Beautiee asked...

"Not here..." Smalls said as he got up, they got up, and they followed Smalls outside...

"I'll call you later..." Smalls said as he got in his car and left...

CHAPTER THIRTEEN

"Good morning..." Sonovia answered...

"May I speak to Sonovia Alexander?" Katina asked...

"Speaking..."

"Ms. Alexander – this is Detective Jones, 3rd Precinct, Milford, Connecticut..."

"How can I help you?"

"I'd like for you and your husband to come in for questioning..."

"For?"

"It's regarding the murders at Mohegan Sun..."

"Do we need an attorney?"

"Not at this time..."

"Not at this time? Ooohhh... okay..."

"Can you come in later today?"

"What time?"

"How's 2 p.m.?"

"We'll be there..." Sonovia said as she hung up...

"What was that about?"

"That was Detective Jones from the 3rd precinct in Milford..."

"Oh shit..."

"They wanna question us Flick! What are we gonna do?"

"Baby..." Flick said as he sat down next to Sonovia... "Calm down..."

"Calm down? The fuck?"

"Baby – here's what we're gonna do..."

"I'm listening..."

"We're gonna tell them the truth..."

"I know you lyin'!"

"Baby – we met him at the casino, we had drinks – we invited him to our room, he started running his mouth, we played cards, I beat his ass, he had to pay me..."

"Hmmm... okay... that'll work..."

"You good?"

"Yea... I'm good..."

"Who the hell is this?" Mary said as she answered the phone in the room... "Good morning..."

"Mary – this is Katina..."

"Yes Katina..."

"I just wanted to let you know Sonovia and her husband are coming in for questioning..."

106

"Really? When?"

"Today at 2..."

"Thank you Katina..." Mary said as she hung up...

"Katina Jones – what did you just do?"

"I set a trap to catch a killer..." Katina answered as she smiled at Beverly...

"Hello – how may I help you?" Jeremy asked...

"We have an appointment to see Detective Jones..." Sonovia answered...

"May I have your names?"

"Flick and Sonovia Alexander..."

"I'll take you to her office..." Jeremy said as they followed him down to her office... "Katina – your 2 p.m. is here..." he said as he stuck his head inside...

"Thank you Jeremy – could you do me a favor and escort her husband to the kitchen while we question his wife?"

"My husband can't be here?"

"No – I'm sorry..."

"Why?"

"It's just procedure..."

"Okay..." Sonovia said as she sat down and Beverly came into office...

"Who's this?" Sonovia asked...

"I'm Beverly Carswell, District Attorney..." she answered...

"Am I under arrest?"

"No... – we just have some questions..." Beverly answered...

"Who's asking the questions?"

"I'll start..." Katina answered as she set up a tripod..."

"This is being recorded?" Sonovia asked...

"Yes..."

"Why is it being recorded if I'm not under arrest?"

"Why are you objecting to it being recorded?" Beverly asked...

"You know what – I'm done..." Sonovia said as she got up...

"Ms. Alexander – we don't have to record it if you don't want us to..." Katina said as she put the tripod down...

"Okay..." Sonovia said as she sat back down...

"I'm going to take notes along with the district attorney..." Katina explained...

"Okay..." Sonovia said...

"I called you and your husband in for questioning because, as you know, Sean Stewart and Aiden Holloway were killed at Mohegan Sun..."

"Okay..."

"We spoke with Mary yesterday..."

"Okay..."

"Mary told us she met you and your husband at I-Hop and you all stayed at the Hyatt in Yonkers – is that correct?"

"Yes – that's correct..."

"Did you know Sean Stewart?"

"Not really..."

"What does that mean?"

"We met Sean at New Resorts in Queens..."

"Were you gambling?"

"We weren't gambling at the time..."

"What do you mean?"

"We were at the bar having drinks when we met Sean – he and my husband hit it off – next thing you know, my husband invited him to our room..."

"What happened in the room?"

"I didn't fuck him!" Sonovia laughed...

"That's not what I'm asking you!" Katina laughed...

"I just wanted to clear that up!" Sonovia laughed...

"What happened in the room?"

"I got into something more comfortable, we had some champagne, Sean started talkin' shit, my husband took out the cards, Sean lost..."

"Are you telling me that Sean was making bets?"

"Yea..."

"Okay – you said Sean lost – so he had to pay your husband?"

"Yea..."

"How did he pay your husband?"

"He transferred the money from his account to mine..."

"You knew where I was going with this I see..."

"Yea... I did..."

"I have something I want to show you..." Katina said as she took the laptop out her desk, opened it up, and started playing the surveillance..."

"Oh shit!" Sonovia exclaimed as she saw Sean entering their room...

"Is that Sean?"

"Yea..."

"Did you invite him to your room?"

"No..." Sonovia whispered as she started crying... "I want my husband..."

"I just have a few more questions..." Katina said as she passed Sonovia some tissues... "Did something happen?"

"I don't wanna talk about it..." Sonovia sniffed as she wiped her nose...

"Sean was angry... he wanted his money back..."

"Yea..."

"I have something else I wanna show you..." Katina said as she began playing more surveillance..."

"Oh shit!" Sonovia exclaimed as she watched the video of Bazil going towards their room...

"Did you invite Bazil Osgood to your room?"

"No..."

"Sonovia... I know you don't wanna talk about what happened – but I need to ask you..."

"I don't wanna talk about it..."

"Did either of these men hurt you?"

"Bazil didn't..."

"So it was Sean then..."

"I don't wanna talk aobut it..."

"You don't have to..." Katina said as she started playing another video...

"Well damn!" Sonovia exclaimed as she watched the surveillance showing her leaving the casino with Bazil...

"Bazil came to the room to check on you... Sean tried to hurt you... Bazil saw that Sean was trying to hurt you... and he took you out of the casino to keep you safe..." Katina said...

"Yea..."

"Okay – I'm finished..." she said as got on the phone... "Jeremy – could you bring her husband in here?"

"Sure..." Jeremy said as he hung up and went to go get Flick. Jeremy brought Flick to Katina's office and when he saw Sonovia, he got angry...

"Why is my wife upset?"

"I'm okay Flick..."

"Babe – no you're not – what the fuck happened?"

"Mr. Alexander – I need you to calm down..." Katina said...

111

"Flick – I'm okay..." Sonovia said...

"Come here..." Flick commanded. Sonovia went over to him and he pulled her into a hug and kissed her... "You sure you're okay?"

"Yea..."

"Ms. Alexander – I need you to come with me while they question your husband..." Jeremy said as he held the door open for her...

"Okay..." Sonovia said as she got up and left with Jeremy...

"Mr. Alexander – may I call you Flick?" Katina asked...

"No you may not – and who are you?" Flick asked as he looked at Beverly...

"I'm Beverly Carswell, District Attorney..." she answered...

"Am I under arrest?"

"No..."

"I'm going to take notes along with the district attorney..." Katina explained...

"Okay..." Flick said...

"I called you and your wife in for questioning because, as you know, Sean Stewart and Aiden Holloway were killed at Mohegan Sun..."

"Okay..."

"We spoke with Mary yesterday..."

"Okay..."

"Mary told us she met you and your wife at I-Hop and you all stayed at the Hyatt in Yonkers – is that correct?"

"Yes – that's correct..."

"Did you know Sean Stewart?"

"We met Sean at Resorts World in Queens..."

"Were you gambling?"

"We met Sean at the bar – we hit it off and I invited him to our room..."

"What happened in the room?"

"Sean started braggin' about how good he was at playin' cards so I took my cards out and I beat his ass!" Flick laughed...

"I bet he was mad..."

"He was – I'd be mad too – but he kept running his mouth – he should 'a quit while he was ahead..."

"Did he pay you?"

"Yea..."

"How did he pay you?"

"He transferred the money from his account to mine..."

"Yours?"

"My wife..."

"I have something I want to show you..." Katina said as she took the laptop out her desk, opened it up, and started playing the surveillance..."

"Oh shit!" Flick exclaimed as he saw Sean entering their room...

"Is that Sean?"

"Yea!"

"Did you invite him to your room?"

"Hell no! Did you show this to my wife? Is this why my wife was upset?"

"Yes..."

"You shouldn't have shown this to her..."

"I had too... I'm sorry..."

"Why?"

"Because we think we know what happened... and this video corroborates what you both said... and it also proves our theory..."

"Your theory? What theory?"

"Sean found out where you were... he was angry... he wanted his money back..."

"Yea..."

"I have something else I wanna show you..." Katina said as she began playing more surveillance..."

"Oh shit!" Flick exclaimed as he watched the video of Bazil going towards their room...

"Did you invite Bazil Osgood to your room?"

"No..."

"Bazil came to your room... he left with Sean... and then he left with your wife..." Katina said as she started playing another video...

"Oh shit!" Flick exclaimed as he watched the surveillance showing his wife leaving the casino with Bazil...

"We know Bazil didn't hurt your wife... but we also know Sean did..."

"How do you know that?" Flick asked...

114

"You just told us he did..." Katina answered as she smiled at Flick. I'm done – thank you for coming in..." she said as she got up...

"That's it? We can go?"

"You can go..."

"You don't have any questions?" Flick asked Beverly...

"I don't have any questions..." Beverly answered. Flick left and went to the kitchen...

"Flick – oh thank God!" she exclaimed when she saw him...

"They know about Sean..."

"How?"

"I fucked up and told them..." Flick sighed as he pulled her into a hug...

"I don't care about that – let's get the fuck outta here..." Sonovia said as she took Flick by the hand and they ran out the precinct...

"Okay Katina – what's next?" Beverly asked...

"I think we have enough evidence to arrest Mary for both murders..." Katina answered...

"Katina... I'm not sure about that..."

"Beverly – she met Sonovia and her husband in Yonkers, they stayed at the same hotel – they wind up at Mohegan Sun – with Sonovia, her husband, Bazil – and the same man that just happens to owe her husband money – that same man winds up dead – her husband winds up dead – and she doesn't check out of the hotel until the next day..."

"Let's wait until we get the report back on the duffel bag they found in the men's room before we make any arrests – I wanna make sure whatever evidence we have we can make it stick..."

"Okay..." Katina agrees as she looks out her office window...

"What are you looking at?"

"I'm watching the fly go into the spider's web..." Katina answered as Beverly came over to the window and they both watched Mary approach Sonovia and Flick in the parking lot...

CHAPTER FOURTEEN

"Snow!" Mary called out when she saw them...

"Mary – what are you doing here?" Sonovia asked...

"Hey Mary..." Flick said...

"Hey – have you guys had lunch?" Mary asked...

"No..." Sonovia answered...

"Me either – let's go get something to eat..."

"Okay – where we goin'?" Flick asked...

"Let's go to Cracker Barrel..."

"Okay... follow us..." Sonovia said as they went to get in the car...

"You okay?" Flick asked...

"Yea – at first I thought I was under arrest – especially when I saw the district attorney..."

117

"I was thinking the same thing..."

"They wanted to record my statement – that Bitch gonna ask me why am I uncomfortable with it being recorded – I said you know what – I'm done!" and I got up...

"Who? Katina?"

"Beverly..."

"Oh yea – I'on like her either –I'on trust her..."

"Me either – but once I knew they weren't recording me I was okay... until I saw that video..."

"I wish they didn't show that to you..."

"Me too..."

"I'm sorry..." Flick said as he took Sonovia's hand and kissed it...

"It's not your fault – it's over now..."

"I wonder what Mary was doing there?"

"I was thinking about that – I'on trust her ass either..."

"Really?"

"I'll see what happens when we get to the restaurant..."

"I can't wait for them to tell me what happened!" Mary exclaimed as she drove... "Shoot – I'm about to find out!" she exclaimed as they pulled in to Cracker Barrel...

"I'm not answering any questions..." Sonovia said...

118

"Me either..." Flick said... as Mary walked up...

"Ready to go inside?" Mary asked...

"Ready..." Flick answered as he put his arm around Sonovia and they went inside...

"Welcome to Cracker Barrel – how many?" the hostess asked...

"Three..."

"Right this way..." the hostess said as she picked up three menus and they followed her...

"I like this view..." Mary said...

"Me too..." Sonovia said...

"I'm glad I ran into you guys..."

"What were you doing at the precinct?" Flick asked...

"I had to drop off something for Katina..." Mary lied... "What were you doing there?"

"Welcome to Cracker Barrel – can I get you some coffee?" the waitress asked as she came over to the table...

"Yes please – I want that caramel macchiato thing..." Sonovia said...

"That sounds good..." Mary said...

"Regular coffee for me..." Flick said...

"Coming right up..." the waitress said as she walked away...

"Let's look at the menu..." Flick suggested, trying to avoid Mary's question...

"What were you doing at the precinct?" Mary asked again...

"Nothing I wanna talk about..." Sonovia sighed...

"That bad huh?"

"Yea..."

"Okay – le'me look at this menu and see what I want to eat..."

"I'm getting breakfast..." Flick said...

"Me too..." Sonovia said..."

"Their breakfast menu does look good..." Mary said..."

"Here's your coffee..." the waitress said as she put the coffee's down on the table... "Are you ready to order?"

"I'm gonna have Uncle Hershcel's Favorite with fried apples and catfish – and extra butter on the grits..." Sonovia answered...

"Got it – next?"

"I'm going to have the Country Morning Breakfast... with fried apples... and sirloin..." Mary answered as she started crying...

"Oh my God – Mary..." Sonovia said as she put her arm around her and held her...

"I'm sorry – it's just..."

"I know..." Sonovia said as she rubbed Mary's back..."

"That's what Aiden used to get..."

"I'm sorry Maam... would you like something else?" the waitress asked...

"It's alright... my husband was killed at the casino..."

"Oh no! I'm sorry for your loss..."

"Thank you..." Mary sniffed...

"What can I get for you?" the waitress asked Flick...

"I'll get Grandpa's Country Fried Breakfast – sausage – with fried apples..."

"Fried eggs or scrambled..."

"Scrambled..." they all answered...

"Okay – I'll be back..." the waitress said as she went to place the order... "I can't wait for her to bring the food back here – I'm hungry!" Mary laughed...

"Here you go..." the waitress said as she began putting the food on the table...

"This looks good!" Flick exclaimed...

"It is..." the waitress agreed as she put the rest of the food on the table...

"Thank you..." Mary said...

"You're welcome – if you need anything else, let me know..." the waitress said as she went to take an order at another table...

"Oh this is so good!" Mary exclaimed...

"It is..." Sonovia agreed. Flick sat there eating without speaking...

"Snow?" Mary asked...

"Yea..." Sonovia answered as she continued eating...

"Please tell me..."

"Tell you what?"

"Tell me why you were at the precinct..." she sighed...

"Oh my God – is that what's bothering you?"

'Yes!"

"They saw me leaving with Bazil..."

"Is that what you were doing there?"

"They call us down there questioning me 'n shit – I told her I didn't fuck him!" Sonovia laughed...

"Oh my God – Flick – what did you say?"

"Nothin' for me to say..." Flick answered as he took a sip of coffee...

"I'm sorry – I just thought... never mind..." Mary sighed...

"You thought they asked me about you..." Sonovia said...

"Yea..."

"They didn't..."

"Hmmm – I guess they really are looking at Bazil then..." Sonovia and Flick looked at each other and smiled behind their coffee...

"How's everything?" the waitress asked...

"Delicious..." Mary answered...

"You see my plate – right?" Flick laughed...

"I see..." the waitress laughed...

"The food was really good..." Sonovia said...

"I'm glad to hear that... here's your check..." she said as she placed it on the table...

"I'll take that..." Flick said as he picked it up... "And you can take this..." Flick said as he placed the tip in her apron pocket..."

"Thank you..." she said as they all got up...

122

"You're welcome..." Flick said...

"I'm going to go back to the hotel and finish your book..." Mary said...

"Are you enjoying it so far?" Sonovia asked...

"I am..."

"Good..."

"Listen – can I call you later?"

"Absolutely..."

"Okay – I'll talk to you later..." Mary said as she went to her car, got in, and drove off...

"You know what she was lookin' for – right?" Flick asked...

"Hell yea I know what she was lookin' for – but she didn't get it..." Sonovia laughed as they got in their car...

"Lyin' mutha fuckas!" Mary exclaimed as she drove off...

"Yes Beverly?" Katina answered...

"The report came back..."

"What did it say?"

"I'll be there in a minute..." Beverly said as she hung up..."

"Le'me see it!" Katina exclaimed...

"Hello to you too!" Beverly laughed... "Here..." she said as she showed Katina the report...

"Inconclusive? Are you fucking kidding me?"

"I'm sorry Katina..." Beverly sighed...

"The hand sanitizer that was used to wipe down the bag contaminated the DNA..." Katina read...

"It doesn't matter – it wasn't Bazil..." Beverly said...

"I know it wasn't – I saw Bazil's foot..."

"You looked at the man's foot?"

"Yea!"

"How can you tell by just looking at his foot?"

"Bazil has a narrow foot – the killer has a wide foot..."

"We still don't know who did it..."

"Let's get Mary back in here for questioning..."

"Why? She didn't kill her husband!"

"I know she didn't – but I wanna tell her the good news..."

"We don't have any good news!" Beverly exclaimed...

"Sure we do – we've confirmed that Bazil isn't a suspect... and we've also confirmed that Mary Holloway is a person of interest..." Katina said as she smiled...

"I guess you're going to call Smalls now?"

"I'll call him..." Katina sighed as she picked up the phone..."

"Yes Katina..." Smalls answered...

"The report came back on the evidence..."

"Okay..."

"It's inconclusive..."

"So you're not looking at my client?"

"We're not looking at your client..."

"Thank you Katina..."

"You're welcome – have a good day..." she said as she hung up...

"Yes Smalls?" Bazil answered as he put the phone on speaker...

"The evidence is inconclusive..."

"Thank you Smalls..."

"You're welcome..." Bazil said as he hung up. Beautiee looked over at Bazil, smiled, and they both went back to whatever they were working on...

CHAPTER FIFTEEN

"Hey Mary..." Sonovia answered...

"Hey Snow..."

"How are you?"

"I'm as good as can be expected..." Mary sighed...

"What are you doing today?"

"I was hoping I could hang out with you..."

"You wanna come to Queens?"

"If you don't wanna be bothered – I understand..." she sighed...

"Le'me send an Uber for you..."

"Snow – you don't have to do that..."

"Yes I do – I don't want you driving drunk..." Sonovia laughed...

"I'm not drunk..." Mary laughed...

"You will be..." Sonovia laughed...

"You know what – that sounds good – I'll get ready..."

"Oh – one more thing..."

"Yes Sonovia..."

"Leave your purse and your phone at the hotel..."

"Why?"

"Once you start drinkin' – you don't need any distractions..."

"Snow – are you trying to have your way with me?" Mary laughed...

"I just want you to be able to relax..."

"Okay Snow... I'll let you know when I'm ready..." Mary said as she hung up. Mary got up from the chair and pulled down her pants... "Come to Mama..." she said as she took the 22 with the holster out of her purse, attached the holster to her thigh, made sure it was secure, put the gun in it, pulled her pants up, and picked up her phone...

"Hello Mary..." Sonovia answered...

"I'm ready..."

"Okay – I'll call you right back..."

"I'll be waiting..."

"Hey Babe..." Flick said as he came into the living room and kissed Sonovia...

"Hey..." she breathed...

"Who was that?"

"That was Mary..."

"How's she doing?"

127

"She's on her way here..."

"She's coming here?!"

"Yea!"

"Why?!"

"Because we have to act like we cool – remember?"

"You right – I'm sorry..."

"I'm sending an Uber for her..."

"Why?" She has a car..."

"Because – if some shit jumps off – she took an Uber because she didn't want to drink and drive..."

"Oh so y'all drinkin'?"

"Yea..."

"Okay..."

"Le'me get this Uber..." Sonovia sighed... "Okay – got it – now I can call Mary..." she said as she called the hotel...

"Yes Snow..."

"Your Uber will be downstairs in 8 minutes..."

"Okay..."

"His name is Fernando – he's driving a White Jeep Grand Cherokee SUV..."

"Okay – le'me get downstairs – I'll see you soon..."

"See you soon..." Sonovia said as she hung up...

"See you soon Flick..." Mary said as she put down her phone, took her coat out the closet, and

128

went downstairs... "There's Fernando..." Mary sighed as he pulled up and she got in...

"Hello Sonovia..." the driver said...

"Hello Fernando..." Mary smiled as she sat back and looked out the window...

"Oh good – she's on her way – it says she'll be here in 20 minutes – I can go to the liquor store and get back before she gets here..." Sonovia said...

"Okay Babe – take your phone with you..."

"I am – I'll be right back..." she said as she headed out. When Sonovia got to the liquor store she got an attitude right away. After she got the liquor, she got on line and called Flick...

"Hey Babe..."

"Flick – can you go downstairs and wait for Mary – I got the liquor but I'm still on line – everybody and their mother decided to come here today..."

"Okay – what's she coming in?"

"A White Jeep Grand Cherokee SUV..."

"Okay – I'm on my way downstairs..." Flick said as he hung up... "There she is..." Flick said as the car pulled up. Flick opened the door for Mary and she got out...

"Thank you Flick..."

"You're welcome – Sonovia went to the liquor store – she'll be back in a few minutes – c'mon..." he said as he put his arm around Mary and walked her towards their house...

"Nice..." Mary said...

"Thank you – we live upstairs..." Flick said as Mary followed him upstairs. When they got upstairs, Flick opened the door and let Mary inside...

"Oh this is nice!" she exclaimed...

"Thank you – let me take your coat..." Mary turned her back to Flick; he took off her coat, and hung it up in the closet... "Have a seat..."

"I'd rather stand..." Mary said as she moved closer to Flick...

"Mary – what are you doing?"

"I finally have you all to myself..." she said as went even closer...

"Umm... Snow will be right back – she don't need to see you tryin' to push up on me..." Flick said as she backed him into the kitchen...

"I've been waiting to do this for a long time..." she said as she dropped her pants...

"Yo – what the fuck – this ain't happening!" Flick exclaimed as Sonovia walked in...

"Oh yes... it's happening..." Mary said as she pulled the 22 out the holster attached to her thigh and pointed it at him...

"Look – I'm sorry about Aiden – I didn't have a choice!" Flick exclaimed as he put up his hands...

"So you admit you killed my husband?" Mary asked as she moved closer. Sonovia tip-

130

toed around the corner and unbeknownst to Mary, she was standing directly in back of her...

"Yes – I killed your husband..."

"Who ordered the hit?" Mary asked as she pointed the gun at Flick's head...

"I did!" Sonovia exclaimed. Mary turned around and was face-to-face with Sonovia... "Put the fuckin' gun down!' Sonovia commanded. Mary dropped the gun to the floor and Sonovia picked it up... "Pull up your pants!" Mary did as she was told... "Get your ass in the bathroom!" she commanded as she pointed down the hall with the gun. Flick came out the corner in the kitchen and followed them both to the bathroom... "Get in the tub!"

"Sonovia – can we talk about this?"

"Bitch – No! Get in the tub!"

"Fine..." Mary sighed as she got in the tub...

"Sit down!" Mary did as she was told... "Flick – get those rubber gloves and put them on..." Flick did as he was told... "Open that cabinet and get those bottles..." Flick opened the cabinet and started taking out the bottles of sulfuric acid...

"No... Sonovia... please... I'm begging you..."

"Bitch – shut the fuck up!"

"Please don't do this – I know I have to die – but not like this..." she pleaded...

"Don't worry – I'll make it quick..." she said as she pointed the 9 millimeter with the silencer on it at Mary's head and pulled the trigger...

"Oh shit! Babe – you planned this?" Flick asked...

"Lay her down in the tub Flick..." Flick did as he was told...

"I was wondering why you kept buying sulfuric acid – I thought you were gonna use it to strip the paint off the walls..." Flick laughed...

"Open them bottles and start pouring them on her body..." Flick did as he was told...

"Pour 'em all in there – make sure her body's covered..." Flick did as he was told...

"Now – we're gonna go inside, have a drink, and wait..."

"Okay Babe..." Flick said as he followed Sonovia into the living room. When they got in the living room, Flick went into the kitchen, made drinks, came back into the living room, handed Sonovia a drink, and sat down. Sonovia took a few sips of her drink before she spoke...

"I ordered the first couple of bottles right after she called me..."

"You did?"

"I knew she didn't come here just to find out what happened to her husband..."

"How'd you know?"

"She was cold..."

"I don't understand..."

"She wasn't the same person we met at I-Hop..."

"I still don't understand how you knew..."

"See – you need to start reading my books again..." she said as Flick finished his drink... "C'mon – let's go clean the bathroom..." she said as she got up and went into the kitchen...

"Why are you goin in the kitchen?"

"Cause we need garbage bags..." she said as she took the garbage bags out the cabinet and then went back into the bathroom...

"Oh shit! It's all liquid!" Flick exclaimed...

"Give me them gloves..." Flick gave Sonovia a pair of rubber gloves and she put them on... "Put your gloves back on, and get that bucket..."

"Okay..." Flick said as he put the gloves on...

"I'm gonna hold the bag open – you scoop that up out the tub and pour it in the bag – we gon' keep doing that until we fill all these bags..."

"We should 'a had some gallon bags..." Flick said as he began scooping and pouring...

"Naa – people see you with gallon bags they get nosey – start asking questions – people see you gin' to the incinerator they just think you got a nasty house..." she laughed as Flick filled the first bag... "I'ma take this out to the incinerator – I'll be right back..." she said as she tied a knot in the bag, picked up one of the empty bottles, picked up the bag, and went out to the incinerator. When she got to the incinerator, she tossed the bottle down first, tossed the bag down, tossed both guns down, closed the door to the incinerator, and went back inside... "Okay – I'm ready for another bag..." she said as she opened another bag...

"Why don't you wait until we finish all the bags?" Flick asked as he scooped..."

"Because I wanna make sure the acid doesn't eat through the bags..." she answered as she tied a knot in the bag... "And people are nosey..." she said as she picked up the bag, picked up another empty bottle, and took it out to the incinerator. They continued this process until they got rid of all the empty bottles and bags... "Now you can throw those gloves in the incinerator when you're done..." she said as she took off her gloves, her clothes, and put them in a garbage bag...

"Aren't you taking that to the incinerator?"

"Naa – you need to clean the bathroom – then you can take your gloves off, take your clothes off, put them in the bag – then you can take it out to the incinerator.." she answered as she put on her robe and slippers...

"Where are you goin'?"

"Shit – I'm tired – I'm goin' to lie down..." she answered as she left him in the bathroom and went into the bedroom...

CHAPTER SIXTEEN

"Jeremy – I'm heading to Bridgeport..." Katina said...

"Okay – I'll let Beverly know..." he said as she left the precinct...

"Hey Katina..." Chandler answered...

"Have you heard from Mary Holloway?"

"No – why?"

"I'm trying to reach her and she's not answering..."

"Have you tried her cell phone?"

"I don't have the number..."

"Hold on – I'll look it up... Holloway – right?"

"Yes..."

"I got it – 475-328-7234..."

"Can you get a location on it?"

"Her last location was Holiday Inn in Bridgeport..."

"Hmmm – maybe she has her phone turned off – thanks Chandler..." she said as she hung up. Katina pulled up in front of the hotel, parked, and went inside...

"Welcome to the Holiday Inn – how may I help you?" Virginia asked...

"I'm looking for a guest..."

"I'll get the Manager..." she said as she went to get the manager...

"Good morning – I'm Mr. Outtaway – how may I help you Detective?"

"You have a Mary Holloway staying at this hotel..."

"What do you need?"

"I haven't been able to reach her..."

"Did you call her?"

"She's not answering..."

"What room is she in?"

"She's in room 313..."

"Come with me..." Mr. Outtaway said as Katina followed him to the elevator and they went upstairs. When they got upstairs, Katina pulled out her gun and went to the door...

"Mary – it's Katina – are you in there?" She listened for an answer and when she didn't get one, she motioned for Mr. Outtaway to unlock the door... "Mary? It's Katina – I'm coming in..." she said as she went in the room and looked around... "Purse is here... phone is here... clothes are here... and your bed hasn't been slept in..." she said as she took out her cell phone...

"Yes Katina..." Chandler answered...

"Meet me at the Holiday Inn, room 313..."

"What happened?!" Chandler exclaimed...

"Mary's missing..."

"I'll be right there!" Chandler said as he hung up...

"I'm Della Crews, Anchor, News 12 Connecticut. We interrupt our regularly scheduled programming to bring you the following news. We now go live to Gwen Edwards. Go ahead Gwen...

"This is Gwen Edwards, Reporter, News 12 Connecticut. We have been communicating with police departments in Bridgeport as well as Milford regarding the deaths of Sean Stewart and Aiden Holloway at Mohegan Sun. News 12 has just confirmed that Mary Holloway has been named as a person of interest in both deaths. We will continue to bring you updates. We now return to our regularly scheduled programming. Back to you Della..."